"Lordy, Lordy, can Lewis Nordan write! . . . N.......
delight and the absolute security we felt as children discovering how
stories can be true and better than true at the same time."

—*Los Angeles Times Book Review*

"Lewis Nordan distinguishes himself not merely for the lyric accuracy of
his prose, for his fine ear for slightly surreal dialog and his eye for the
startling detail, but for being a Mississippi writer of whom one can say
with relief: 'He does *not* plow the same field as Faulkner.'"

—*The Memphis Commercial Appeal*

"Because *Music of the Swamp* is radiant with much that we have been missing, because it tells us what we can stand to withstand and yet survive, it
should not be missed. Listen to its music." —*Baton Rouge Sunday Advocate*

"Nordan's engaging, wise, delightfully wry stories sound a melodious, bittersweet yawp, pulsating with love, grief, rage and a thirst for redemption."

—*Publishers Weekly*

"Lewis Nordan's wonderful *Music of the Swamp* lyrically conjures up a
Southern-fried childhood that's as dark, hilarious and affecting as any
you're likely to encounter." —*The Cleveland Plain Dealer*

"A wild boogie-woogie ride, ranging up and down the scale from broad
humor to the worst heartbreak." —*Asheville Citizen-Times*

"Nordan introduces a group of characters as wild and woolly, as unpre-
dictable, outrageous and violence-prone as the land that spawns them."

—*Chicago Tribune*

"[Sugar Mecklin] rides . . . on the wings of what must be the most active,
troubled and complex preadolescent imagination in American fiction."

—*The Raleigh News and Observer*

"Nordan brings wit, warmth, elegance, grace, and an original, persuasive love [to] his hidebound, inarticulate characters." —*Kirkus Reviews*

"Lewis Nordan is one of those southern writers who provoke a cringe of pain right after the belly laugh. His books . . . are very funny and deep-down sad, stirring up great heaps of emotion." —*New York Newsday*

"*Music of the Swamp* defies easy synopsis, but that's exactly why its worth reading." —*Arkansas Gazette*

"*Music of the Swamp* is a song worth listening to. It will call you back to your own childhood." —*The Jackson Clarion-Ledger*

"Lewis Nordan . . . creates in Sugar Mecklin a complex personality who alternately trusts and doubts, and then fabricates what can't be known. He is the unreliable narrator who makes you want to believe." —*Greensboro News and Record*

"It's a winner." —*The Orlando Sentinel*

"The *Music of the Swamp* in Lewis Nordan's third book of fiction is a tortured, bluesy refrain, a bittersweet melody syncopated with sadness relieved by moments of all-too-human comedy." —*The Atlanta Journal-Constitution*

"Mr. Nordan's fiction is indeed magical, suffused with humor and death . . . [He] has written a wonderful book." —*The Dallas Morning News*

"*Music of the Swamp* is a funny and sad and troubling book. In Nordan's skillful hands facts become slippery, magical, humorous, and black." —*The Houston Post*

"Nordan is not walking on the earth. The man is writing out of the earth. There is a very physical reality about Nordan's characters and settings. Nothing is mere adornment. Everything is of the mud of the earth. He is a swampy sort of writer that is so rare today." —*The Pittsburgh Press*

# Music of the Swamp

## Also by Lewis Nordan

# Music of the Swamp

## Lewis Nordan

Algonquin Books of Chapel Hill   1992

Grateful acknowledgement is made to the *Southern Review,* the PEN Fiction Awards, National
Public Radio, *Story,* the *Chattahoochee Review,* and the *Southern Humanities Review,* where some of
these stories first appeared. And thanks also to the Pennsylvania Council for Arts for two
summer grants.

Algonquin Books of Chapel Hill
PO Box 2225, Chapel Hill, North Carolina 27515-2225
a division of Workman Publishing
225 Varick Street, New York, New York 10014

First Front Porch Paperbacks Edition, September 1992. Originally published in hardcover
by Algonquin Books of Chapel Hill in 1991.

"Muddy Water," words by Jo Trent, music by Peter De Rose & Harry Richman, copyright
© 1926 (Renewed) by Music Sales Corporation & Fred Fisher Music. International copyright secured. All rights reserved. Used by permission.

"Honeycomb," written by Bob Merrill, copyright © 1953, 1982 by Golden
Bell Songs. All rights reserved. Used by permission.

LIBRARY OF CONGRESS CATALOGING-IN-PUBLICATION DATA
Nordan, Lewis.
Music of the swamp / Lewis Nordan.
p. cm.
ISBN 978-0-945575-76-4 (HC)
I. Title.
PS3564.O55M8 1991
813'.54-dc20 91-7777 CIP

ISBN 978-1-56512-016-7 (PB)

10 9 8 7 6 5 4

*For Alicia*

Take away the arrogance, the battery, and the alcohol, and down comes innocence.

—*Judy Grahn*

# PART I

# Music of the Swamp

THE INSTANT Sugar Mecklin opened his eyes on that Sunday morning, he believed that this was a special day and that something new and completely different from anything he had ever known before was about to jump out at him from somewhere unexpected, a willow shade, a beehive, a bird's nest, the bream beds in Roebuck Lake, a watermelon patch, the bray of the iceman's mule, the cry of herons in the swamp, he did not know from where, but wherever it came from he believed it would be transforming, it would open up worlds to him that before today had been closed. In fact, worlds seemed already to be opening to him.

When he later came into the kitchen and sat down to his Sunday breakfast of chocolate milk and homemade bread, toasted and smeared with sweet butter and fresh cinnamon, his mother noticed a difference in Sugar and placed her hand against his forehead and said, "Are you running a fever?"

And then when Sugar's father came into the room, Sugar leaped up out of his chair and did what he had never done before, he grabbed his father suddenly around the neck and hugged him and said, "I love you, Daddy."

This is the kind of day it was. This is the way Sugar Mecklin's summer morning started out.

First there were the mice. Sugar was still asleep when he heard them singing. Sugar was dreaming that he was standing alone in the shade of tupelo gums and cypress and chinaberry and weeping willow and mimosa and that the water of Roebuck Lake was exactly as it was in real life, slick and opaque as a black mirror, with the trees and high clouds reflected perfectly in the surface. He dreamed that he walked out to the end of a short pier, the one that in real life he had built, and saw a beautiful creature of some kind, a mermaid maybe, rise up from the water. Her breasts were bare, and she was singing directly to him as she combed her long hair with a comb the color of bone, and in the other hand held a mirror as dark and fathomless as the mirror-surface of Roebuck Lake.

He believed that this creature could foretell his future, or endow him with power and knowledge. There seemed little wonder to Sugar Mecklin, waking up to such thoughts, that this day should turn out to be special.

And then once he was awake, there was Elvis. Until this very morning Sugar Mecklin had never before heard the name of Elvis Presley. And now here he was, this Elvis person, in full uh-huh complaint on Sugar's Philco radio, and he seemed truly to be singing about the dream that Sugar Mecklin had just dreamed. Elvis told Sugar *you'll be so lonely you could die.*

It was as if the mermaid's song had come to him first

through the sweet voices of the mice in his mattress and then from WMC in Memphis.

These were the reasons Sugar Mecklin astonished his father at the breakfast table by grabbing him suddenly and holding onto him for all he was worth and almost actually saying, pleading, Don't ever leave me, Daddy, I'll be so lonely I will die.

He did not actually say these words, he said only, "I love you, Daddy!" in a bright voice, and his father struggled and finally muttered, "Good luck on your travels through life," and then went out to the garage to get paint buckets and brushes and dropcloths and a stepladder to paint the bathroom, which had needed painting for a long time, probably.

And then after breakfast, while Sugar Mecklin's father spread paint and Sugar Mecklin's mother ran cold water through a colander full of figs to be put up in paraffin-sealed Mason jars as purpley preserves, Sugar Mecklin thought it might not be a bad idea at all to comb his hair with Wildroot Cream Oil and put on his hightop tennies and take a walk right down the middle of Lonely Street and stand along the shore of dark, wooded Roebuck Lake and look across its waters in search of barebreasted women. It was a day in which such a thing might happen, he believed.

His mother said, "Are you going to Sunday school this morning, Sugar?"

Sugar Mecklin said, "Haven't decided."

His mother said, "I wish you would put on a clean shirt and go to Sunday school once in a while."

Not today. Today was a Sunday, this was a whole summer, in fact, in which magic might prove once and for all to be true. It was a summer in which Sugar Mecklin noticed many things, as if they had not been there before, like the mice in his mattress, like Elvis Presley on the Philco. This summer Sugar Mecklin heard the high soothing music of the swamp, the irrigation pumps in the rice paddies, the long whine and complaint, he heard the wheezy, breathy asthma of the compress, the suck and bump and clatter like great lungs as the air was squashed out and the cotton was wrapped in burlap and bound with steel bands into six-hundred-pound bales, he heard the operatic voice of the cotton gin separating fibers from seeds, he heard a rat bark, he heard a child singing arias in a cabbage patch, he heard a parrot make a sound like a cash register, he heard the jungle rains fill up the Delta outside his window, he heard the wump-wump-wump-wump-wump of biplanes strafing the fields with poison and defoliants, he read a road sign that said WALNUT GROVE IS RADAR PATROLLED and heard poetry in the language, he heard mourning doves in the walnut trees.

And for a moment, when he arrived at the edge of the water, Sugar Mecklin almost believed that he had found whatever magical thing he had come looking for.

When he looked across the water to the spot where in his dream he had seen the woman admiring her own reflection in a black mirror, he heard clear sweet tuneful voices raised in plaintive anthems to God in heaven.

There was a cow, a brown-and-white heifer with horns, standing chest-deep in the water directly across the lake. The cow was not supposed to be there, it had only wandered there and could not be coaxed out of the water in time, and so it only stood and once or twice flicked its tail against invisible insects that may have been flying in the morning air.

All about the cow were men and women in white robes—black persons, colored people, Negroes, whatever they were called—and they too, like the cow, were standing chest-deep in the water, and it was their voices that Sugar Mecklin heard in song.

It was a baptizing. *I come to the garden alone* the voices said, in complaint as profound as Elvis Presley's uh-huh *and the voice I hear falling on my ear* the singers sang, speaking of Jesus, who would take away loneliness.

The song went on, and then when it finished there were other songs, questions—*shall we gather at the river*, the singers wanted to know *the beautiful, the beautiful river*—and in a way all of the songs were about loneliness, and the defeat of loneliness, and the heartbreak if it could not be defeated, as probably it never could *you'll be so lonely you could die*

And so this was the happiest moment Sugar Mecklin had

ever felt in his life. He was almost delirious with strong feeling. His face was flushed and even in the Mississippi heat he was almost cold, almost shivering with emotion. The sweat beads on his arms were like a thin film of ice.

And then another child showed up.

Sugar Mecklin was startled. It was Sweet Austin. Where had Sweet Austin come from, so unexpectedly? Sugar Mecklin thought Sweet Austin looked a little like he had seen a ghost.

Sweet said, "Hey, Sugar Mecklin."

Sugar said, "Hey, Sweet Austin."

Sweet Austin walked out onto the narrow pier and stood behind Sugar, and for a minute or two neither of them said anything. Sugar and Sweet were the only two completely white-haired, blue-eyed, freckle-faced, skinny-assed boys in their whole class. People thought it was funny that they looked so much alike and their names were almost the same, Sugar and Sweet.

They only stood and watched the baptizing. *oh what needless pain we bear* sang the choir on the other side of the lake.

Sugar Mecklin said, "You know about a singer name of Elvis Presley?"

Sweet Austin said, "Hey, Sugar . . ."

Sugar Mecklin said, "He sings this song about Heartbreak Hotel."

Sweet Austin said, "Hey, Sugar, listen . . ."

Sugar Mecklin said, "His voice, this guy Elvis Presley's

voice . . ." Sugar didn't know exactly what he was going to say about Elvis Presley's voice. That it made you visible to yourself and invisible to others.

Sweet Austin said, "I've got to show you something. Something bad."

Something was definitely wrong with Sweet Austin. Sweet Austin had definitely seen a ghost.

Across the lake the choir had a friend in Jesus. God's grace was amazing, they said, and sweet. There was a church in the wildwood, they said, and their voices floated across the lake to the pier where Sugar and Sweet were standing and the voices reached them like angels' voices and invited them to come to the church in the wildwood, come to the church in the dell, whatever a dell was, it might be like a swamp, mightn't it, or a bog, or a quicksand pit, what the hell was a dell, anyway?

Just then the brown-and-white cow decided it was time to leave the water and, as the choir sang a final song—*oh I'm tired and so weary but I must travel on*—the cow, as if it had been waiting for just this moment in the music, opened its amazing and sweet old cow-mouth and hollered one long heartbreaking bellow and moan, one incredible tenor note in perfect tune and time with the rest of the choir, as if to impart some message about hope, or maybe hopelessness and loneliness, who could tell the difference, or maybe just to say goodbye I've had enough of this, these horseflies and this sentimental music are driving me crazy, and then turned and slogged its way past the robed communicants and out of the water and up the muddy bank and into the pasture towards a barn.

*there'll be no sadness,* the choir sang, *no sorrow, no trouble . . .* and Sugar knew that when you say these things what you really mean is that sadness and sorrow are all there is and all there ever will be. And then somebody, a young woman in a white robe, waded forth, chest-deep in the black water, and allowed herself to be dunked backwards, out of sight, by a white-haired Negro woman, who held her hand over the young woman's face in the name of the Father and the Son and the Holy Ghost and held that young woman beneath the water for a long time while catfish and cottonmouths and snapping turtles joined with Christ Our Lord to wash away all her sins in the dear sweet magical blood of the Lamb while the choir sang songs.

Sweet Austin said, "I was running trotlines and found it. You've got to come with me."

SWEET AUSTIN had come here in a boat. That was how he had appeared so unexpectedly behind Sugar Mecklin on the pier. When they had walked down the lake bank for a few yards, Sugar saw the boat pulled up in the weeds in a clear spot between the cypress knees. They crawled into the boat, first Sugar Mecklin, up front, and then Sweet Austin in back. Sugar looked out across the lake at the shanties and pulpwood along the ridge on Runnymeade plantation, where the Negroes lived.

Sweet Austin stuck a Feather paddle into the gummy leaf-moldy bottom of the lake and used the paddle like a raft pole to shove the boat away from the bank and to ease them out into the deeper water.

Sweet Austin said to Sugar Mecklin, "I don't know what to do, tell me what to do, Sugar. If I had a daddy I would know what to do."

For one second, when Sugar Mecklin spotted the bare feet and legs sticking up out of the water, he managed to believe that Sweet Austin had brought him here to see the mermaid. He knew better, of course. He knew this was a dead person.

They were far down the lake now. White cranes stood in small gossipy groups along the shallow water near the Runnymeade side of the shore. Turkey vultures sailed like hopeful prayers above them in the wide blue sky and then settled into the empty branches of white-trunked leafless trees. Deep in the water there were fish everywhere, invisible to Sugar Mecklin, no one could know how many of them, bream and perch and bass, silver and gold and blue, and for the first time in his life the thought of hidden fish and all their familiar coloration and feathery gills and lidless eyes terrified Sugar, he could not say why.

It was a body, of course, snagged upside down in a drift of brush.

Now here is the oddest thing. When Sugar Mecklin saw the naked legs poking up out of the water, he thought first of his daddy in speckled overalls back at the house, standing on the fourth rung of a stepladder and holding a bucket and brush and smearing paint over the bathroom ceiling.

Sugar Mecklin said, "Turn the boat around, Sweet Austin. We got to tell somebody. We got to call Big Boy Chisholm."

The body was an old man, it turned out, who may have had a seizure of some kind before he went into the water. Later on, his boat was found with a fishing rod and baited hooks in the floorboards. There were two catfish still alive on a stringer hooked to the side of the boat. The old man had been missing for a couple of days—he lived on Runnymeade with his daughter. The daughter, the *Greenwood Commonwealth* reported, had told her father not to go out on the lake by himself, because he had "spells."

Sweet Austin and Sugar Mecklin did not know all this yet. They only knew that there were legs and feet sticking up out of the drift, and so they did the only thing they could do. Sweet Austin dragged the paddle behind the boat in a sculling motion and turned them in the direction of a camp-landing a little farther on, near the town dump where the rats were as big as yellow dogs and howled all night at the moon. Sweet Austin dipped the paddle deep into Roebuck and caused the boat beneath them to move steadily across the lake to Raney's fish camp, where somebody would let them use the telephone to call Big Boy Chisholm, the lawman.

When they docked at the fish camp, Mr. Raney made the call for them, though it took him a while to find his glasses and even after he did find them he dialed the wrong number four times. Each time he said, "I. Godfrey," and then dialed again. He said, "Y'all just get yourself a Co-Cola out of the icebox." He said, "Are y'all boys all right now?"

Sugar Mecklin and Sweet Austin said that they thought so, they thought they were all right. They looked at one another to decide whether this was true.

Mr. Raney said, "Y'all boys look enough alike to be sisters." This was Mr. Raney's kind way of making a dead man in the swamp a little less horrible idea than it actually was.

Mr. Raney was the last man in Arrow Catcher, Mississippi, who could spit into a brass spittoon from a long distance. He did this now. Ptooey! Pting! He did this as a way of thinking things out. Or maybe only to make a joke, nobody knew which. Ptooey! Pting!

A young man named Hydro—it was Mr. Raney's own son, his only child—who had a big head on his shoulders and a peach pie in his lap, sat down in Mr. Raney's high-backed rocker and rocked so far backwards he turned the pie upside down and nearly turned himself over in the chair, and said, "Shit far and save matches!" Hydro often chased cars and howled when the firetruck turned on the siren and had to be given ice cream so that he would stop.

Then several more times, Mr. Raney spat in rapid succession, ptooey pting! ptooey pting! ptooey pting! while Sugar Mecklin and Sweet Austin shifted from one foot to the other and listened to somebody pull the crank rope on an old Evinrude and start up the rattly little engine down by the dock, where it idled for now, smelling of gasoline and warm oil, and waiting for Big Boy Chisholm to show up so somebody could help steady him while he got into the boat and then lead him down Roebuck Lake to the brush pile where he would collect the corpse.

Mr. Raney said, "Hydro, get your lazy no-count ass out of my rocking chair, or I'll pistol-whip you within an inch of your worthless life."

Hydro was eating his mama's peach pie with a big steel spoon—he had gotten the deep dish turned upright again and had not lost much of the pie—and he did not hear his daddy just then, so Mr. Raney just blew his nose hard into a red bandana and said, "I. Godfrey," and let the matter drop, what good did it do to argue, what difference did it make anyway.

To Sugar Mecklin and Sweet Austin, Mr. Raney said, "We're all going to be a little edgy for a while, it don't mean nothing. It's normal after you find a floater."

Sweet Austin did not go to his own home that night. He couldn't do that. Sweet Austin's mama would be working late behind the bar at the American Legion Hut. She would turn on the switch that caused the Miller High Life sign to revolve. She would scatter sawdust on the little hardwood dance floor for whoever might want to take a turn to the music. She would reach into the cooler for long-necked beers in dark bottles, maybe Pabst Blue Ribbon, or Falstaff, or Jax, or even Pearl, and crack them open with a church key and say to men wearing bunion pads on their feet and Vitalis in their hair, "You don't want no glass with that, do you, loverboy?"

She might take a shot of Early Times herself and chase it down with a swig from one of those men's long-neck bottles, and then peel the label for him. She might belch real loud and make all the men in the Legion Hut laugh and make all the women think she was common. She might sing a song, too, if anybody asked her. She might sing "Honeycomb" if she felt like it, she might sing *honeycomb won't you be my baby oh honeycomb be my own just a hank of hair and a piece of bone my honeycomb* Her arms would be tired and cold and maybe numb from the ice chest and from weariness and loneliness because her man was dead, or she hoped he was anyway, and her apron would smell like the stale beer and cigarettes and her fingers would be crinkly from being wet all night, when she got home and finally found the light switch in the hall and scared the cockroaches off the counters and back up into the kitchen cabinets where they belonged, and staggered a little in the hallway, where she finally propped herself up and took off her shoes.

She might go into the room where her son slept on an army cot and wake up Sweet Austin and tell him what a no-count scoundrel his daddy was, and always had been, and she might tell Sweet Austin he was just like his daddy, just ee-zackly like him, and then she might crawl in right alongside Sweet Austin on the army cot and fall asleep and wake up full of re-grets and no energy to apologize to her boy or to anybody else.

Or she might not come home at all that night, that was surely a possibility, a distinct possibility she herself might say, not if Al the Boogie Woogie Piano Player, who had two gold teeth in the front of his mouth and silver taps on his shoes, asked her to go somewhere with him after they turned off the lights of the Legion Hut and unplugged the slot machines and washed the last beer glasses and re-bagged the last of the pret-zels and beernuts, especially if he asked her to go riding with him in his Oldsmobile, with the rag top down on this warm summer night and maybe kiss a few hard, whiskey-breathed kisses beneath the Confederate memorial.

She might sleep that night in Al the Boogie Woogie Piano Player's bed where he lived for now in a damp room of the Arrow Hotel, and she might feel just so damn awful after she got there and got her stockings off at long last, that she couldn't sleep and so she might ask Al to sing her a baby lul-laby to help her drift off, she might ask him to sing a song she remembered from her own girlhood, on a record that she sneaked around to play on a wind-up Victrola, a song called

"Let These Red Lips Kiss Your Blues Away," and Al might actually know the song, since he knew every song in this bad world, but he would be too tired to sing it, and so Sweet Austin's mama might have to go to sleep without it, it didn't matter, she had gone to sleep sick and lonely plenty of times before, what difference would one more time make, none, it wouldn't make any difference at all to anybody, why should it.

And so Big Boy Chisholm dropped the two boys off at Sugar Mecklin's house. Big Boy didn't turn on the siren today—the whistle, he always called it—or the revolving light on top of the car, though normally he did when he gave a child a ride home. Today he only drove them from the fish camp and stopped the car out by the iron fence in front of Sugar's house and said, "I'm sorry y'all boys had to bear witness to that floater, I truly am sorry." He waited until the two boys had left the car and slammed their doors good and were clear of the road and out of harm's way and up under the catalpa trees, which were covered in locust husks, and past the iron hitching posts in the shape of black horses, and then Big Boy Chisholm drove away in his car, real slow, down Lake Front Road.

It was late in the afternoon now. Bessie Smith was on the phonograph, so that meant that Sugar Mecklin's daddy was already drunk. Sugar Mecklin's daddy called his Bessie Smith records his wrist-cutting music. It was Bessie Smith singing a long time ago when Gilbert Mecklin stuck the ice pick in his chest. *my mama says I'm reckless* Bessie Smith had sung that day, and he knew just what she meant too, he was reckless too. *my daddy says I'm wild* Bessie Smith sang. Nobody knew better than Gilbert Mecklin what it meant to be reckless and wild. Nobody in this world. *I ain't good looking* she sang *but I'm somebody's angel child* Bessie Smith had been singing that day before Sugar Mecklin was even born. In a way that was the good old days, Gilbert Mecklin remembered them fondly, that day long time ago when he had let the record play to its end and then jammed an ice pick straight into his breast bone.

Sugar Mecklin had heard all about it, and he couldn't help wishing that Bessie Smith was not on the phonograph on this particular day. He wished instead that his daddy had waited until after Sugar had had time to come home and say, "Me and Sweet found a dead man. Can Sweet sleep over tonight?" before he started playing wrist-cutting music.

And, if the truth be knew—this was a phrase that Gilbert Mecklin used and drove Sugar's mama straight out of her last and only mind, "if the truth be knew"—Gilbert Mecklin was just this minute saying to himself, he his ownself would have preferred not to be drunk this afternoon. If the truth be knew, Gilbert Mecklin was sitting there in his chair thinking, Now I wonder how this happened again, just when I didn't want it to happen, how did it come to pass that I am sitting here unintentionally drunk on my ass with wrist-cutting music playing on the record player when I have great need to comfort two children who have lost so much and seen too much death in their little lives? The alcohol made Gilbert Mecklin groggy. He felt a little like he had been hit over the head and covered with a heavy blanket.

On the phonograph now there was a trombone. It started way down low, and it could have been the voice of a Texas longhorn cow at first, or an alligator in a swamp quartet singing bass, it was so low. Gilbert Mecklin listened to it. He had to. Nobody else knew how to listen to it. His wife sure hell didn't know how to listen to music. She didn't appreciate music. The trombone note was rising now, rising up and up. Listen to that clear note rise up from the muddy waters of the Delta!

Sugar Mecklin and Sweet Austin were standing in the doorway of Gilbert's bedroom, trying to tell him about the body.

Gilbert already knew about the body. Big Boy Chisholm had called him from the fish camp, had told him Sweet Austin was coming to spend the night. He didn't need to hear about the body.

Sugar said, "Hey, Daddy."

Well, the thing was, after the trombone note got up in the air high enough, it started to blend in with another horn, a trumpet maybe, that took up the note and brought it up even higher, headed up to the moon, until another note got inside these two, a clarinet, so high it was a squeak, like the sound at the tail end of a long crying spell, and then, well, Gilbert Mecklin couldn't very well say hey to Sugar right this very minute, because now Bessie Smith was right there in the room with him, talking to him about his whole life.

*Dixie moonlight, Shawnee shore* Bessie Smith said to Gilbert Mecklin. She seemed to be sitting right there on the bed beside his two boys. She had only one leg, she lost the other leg in Clarksdale, the night she was killed. Oh those sad brass horns, like a crying child. Bessie Smith said she was *headed homebound just once more* she said she was going to her Missy-Sippy Delta home. The trumpet was still there, but now it had a mute on it, and it was weeping real tears. Oh yes, it was a good thing Sugar Mecklin's mama had thrown that ice pick up under the house all those years ago, this was a song that took a man back to better days.

Sugar said, "Me and Sweet Austin found a dead man, Daddy."

Gilbert Mecklin said, "Hush, hush up, Sugar. Listen to this song."

Gilbert had not meant to say this. The last thing in the world he meant to do was tell his boy to hush up. What he meant to say was that there was just so much death in the Delta, it was everywhere, he didn't know how a child could stand all of it. He meant to tell Sweet Austin that he had known Sweet's daddy—if Curtis Austin really was Sweet's daddy, who knows about this kind of thing, who can ever really know for sure—he had known Curtis well and one time watched him play semi-pro ball for the Greenwood Dodgers, a

farm team for Brooklyn, where he played second base and got
three hits that night under the lights. He meant to say that
Sweet Austin's daddy was not an evil man, not completely, and
was still alive, Gilbert knew this, and believed in his heart
that he was doing the right thing by staying out of Sweet and
his mama's life.

Sweet Austin said, "Hey, Mr. Mecklin."

Gilbert Mecklin said, "Hush up, Sweet Austin. Listen
here, listen to this here song."

The music played, and Bessie Smith sang on, and the Delta
was bad, bad, she was saying, and it was magic, it hypnotized
you, you couldn't resist it even if you tried, and now it was
calling her back. *I hear those breezes a-whispering* she complained
*I hear those breezes a-whispering come on back to me*

Gilbert Mecklin wanted to tell these two boys, one of them
his own boy, and the other one, well God knows, Sweet Austin, only God knows—so, Lord, anyway, he wanted to tell
them that there are worse things in this world than bodies in
the swamp, and worse things than having a daddy who died
there, or who ran off and left you, or didn't run off but just left
you anyhow, there are worse things than being so lonely you
could die. If you were real unlucky you could turn into one of
those daddies who left.

Sugar Mecklin said, "Daddy, we saw the feet and legs."
Sugar and Sweet were sitting on the edge of Gilbert Mecklin's
bed, right next to Bessie Smith. Though Bessie Smith was

black and a long time dead and had only one leg, the three of them looked enough alike to be wild and frightened sisters.

Sweet Austin said, "Lodged up in a drift. I was running trotlines, I didn't know what to do."

In a way it was a good thing that Gilbert Mecklin was so drunk right now, really it was, it wasn't a completely bad thing to be so drunk if you looked at it in the right light. Drunk like this, he didn't have to tell these two scared boys what it meant to have chickens in his back yard, Plymouth Rocks and Rhode Island Reds, the layers and bantams and the blue Andalusian rooster. He didn't have to say that when he walked out there and scattered shelled and fragrant corn from an enameled dishpan, one slow handful at a time, he could forget his own father, who spent all his family's pennies for shoes made of kangaroo leather and for Havana cigars and then beat him and his brother with fists and sticks and straps and then, worst of all, went blind for spite and had to be waited on hand and foot for the rest of his life.

And so Bessie Smith just kept on singing about the Delta. In fact she was singing about Arrow Catcher, Mississippi. She was singing about Roebuck Lake, right near where she died that rain-swole-up Delta summer in a crash on the highway and lost one of her legs. *muddy water 'round my feet* Bessie Smith was saying, and right now all of a sudden it wasn't Gilbert Mecklin she was singing to, it was Sweet Austin, who didn't know she didn't have feet, only one foot, there on the edge of the bed, like it was the edge of a cliff and he might fall off.

Bessie Smith was telling him what he already knew. You are trapped here, Sweet Austin, we all are. It don't help to have a daddy, you're trapped anyway, daddies will always leave, always die, always be somebody you don't know. Daddies ain't your trouble, Sweet Austin. Your trouble is the geography. You better learn to like it. Bessie Smith said there was *muddy water 'round my feet muddy water in the street* She said *just God's own shelter down on the Delta*

Sweet Austin knew about Sugar Mecklin's daddy and the ice pick. He said, "Mr. Mecklin, how come you want to listen to wrist-cutting music?"

Bessie Smith said *muddy water in my shoes*

Gilbert Mecklin looked and saw that Bessie Smith was not really sitting on the bed beside the two boys. Well, that was good anyway.

Way back behind Bessie Smith was a slow piano. Just one chord, and then her strong sad voice and then another chord, like punctuation. Sweet Austin thought of Al the Boogie Woogie Piano Player, he thought of the Oldsmobile and his mama's hair blowing in the Delta breeze. There was a one-note clarinet back there too, as slow as the piano, like an old, old, one-trick pony. Yikes! the clarinet said, like a sad swamp bird, and yes yes yes.

Sugar Mecklin's mama came into the room now. She said, "Gilbert, don't fill these boys' heads with drunk-talk. They're worth more than that."

Sugar Mecklin loved his mama's hairbrushes and bobby pins and facial creams, he loved her clean underwear in a drawer. He was glad she wasn't a floozie like Sweet Austin's mama, he was glad he didn't have to come home at night and wonder if she was sharing a room with Al the Boogie Woogie Piano Player at the Arrow Hotel, he was glad she never slipped into bed beside him and slept drunk all night.

Bessie Smith said *muddy water in my shoes, rocking in them lowdown blues* The piano, the squeaky old-fashioned one-trick-pony clarinet, and now one low and rising note from the trombone, like a good memory. And just then Sugar Mecklin started to know something that he had not quite known before. He knew that he was not all alone in the world after all, as he had for so long believed.

There was his mama, who always seemed sane in comparison with his daddy who was not sane at all. She was out of her mind with old grief, old loss, her own tyrannical father, her fat brother who could not get out of his bed for fear of lightning. She hated music, she secretly broke and threw away Gilbert's favorite records, one at a time while he was drunk, especially "Summertime," which seemed to Mrs. Mecklin an affront to everything decent—those first three high-squealing notes of self-pity and false sentiment—and which Sugar found in a million ragged pieces of plastic out by the chicken-yard fence. She dreamed of trains crossing frozen landscapes, she made up stories of escape, using models in the Sears, Roebuck catalog for characters to represent herself and her fictional friends, she pretended she grew up as a serving girl in Canada and that for spare pennies she made beaded bags, huddled over her georgette-stretched beading frame, her fingers feeding beads and thread to her crochet needle like lightning.

And there beside him was Sweet Austin, who looked enough like himself to be his sister, and who looked enough like Gilbert Mecklin to be his, his, well, God only knows what. The world was not what Sugar Mecklin wanted it to be, but he was not alone, he would never be alone.

Bessie Smith said *I don't care, it's muddy there, but it's still my home*

Sweet Austin said, "What was so bad, Mr. Mecklin, was, like, I seen them bare legs poking up out of the water and I thought it was my daddy. I knowed it wont, but I thought it was."

Bessie Smith was wailing now, weeping in song *I don't care, I don't care, it's still my home* The muted trumpet was back and it was crying like a baby.

Gilbert said, "Naw, Sweetness, it wont your daddy." The alcohol was beginning to wear off a little. Gilbert Mecklin felt a little less bushwhacked than before. Maybe he better have one more drink, just so he don't get sick. Maybe he would, maybe he wouldn't.

Mrs. Mecklin sat down on the bed beside Sweet Austin and put her arms around his neck, and Sweet Austin leaned into her shoulder and started to cry. Sweet Austin was a big boy, a little taller than Sugar and maybe a little broader shouldered. When did that happen, Sugar wondered, when did he start to outgrow me? Sugar Mecklin felt funny sitting there and looking at this young man holding his mama and his mama holding him tighter than he himself had ever been held. They rocked back and forth to Sweet Austin's crying and to the sad old bluesy sentimental music.

Bessie Smith said *got my toes turned Dixie way*

Mrs. Mecklin said, "You just cry now, Sweetness, you just go right on and cry."

Bessie Smith said *'round the Delta let me lay*

Sweet Austin was really going at it now. He was boo-hooing flat out. Boo hoo, boo hoo, boo-fucking-hoo, man. He was getting snot in Mrs. Mecklin's hair. It didn't matter. It didn't matter to anybody, not even Sugar.

Mrs. Mecklin said, "Your mama loves you to death, Sweet Austin. And so does your daddy."

Gilbert Mecklin was wondering if he might risk getting up just this minute and easing into the kitchen for another nip of that Old Crow, just to settle his stomach.

Sweet Austin and Mrs. Mecklin were rocking and reeling now, slow, slow. Mrs. Mecklin was whispering like a mama. She said, "And me and Gilbert love you too, Sweetness. We love you like you was our own boy."

Yessir, no doubt about it, Gilbert Mecklin could certainly use another drink.

So that's what he did. He stood up and steadied himself beside his chair and then eased on out towards the kitchen, just so he didn't mess around and get sick from having an empty stomach. Maybe a beer would settle him down some. The carbonation, the food value. Maybe a shot of Old Crow would taste good with it.

Sweet Austin cried. Mrs. Mecklin sang him a soft baby lullaby. Sugar Mecklin believed he was a part of a family, and this filled him with love.

The world was not the way Sugar Mecklin wanted it to be, but he had to admit, this particular day had turned out even better than he had expected when he woke up to the sound of mice and Elvis Presley and the voice of a barebreasted woman singing into a black mirror.

Bessie Smith said *my heart cries out for muddy water*

# PART II

# Cabbage Opera

THERE WAS a man named McNeer who lived in my hometown of Arrow Catcher, Mississippi. I saw him only infrequently, though I knew his wife and two children. Mr. McNeer worked all night in a Rose Oil service station in a town ten miles away, and so he was rarely visible around the house. The four of them lived near the school, at the end of a cotton field in a pre-fab shack with peeling yellow paint. Mrs. McNeer operated a little store on the same property. The store had a gas pump and a few groceries, and she made pimento-cheese sandwiches to sell to school children at lunchtime.

The McNeers had a son a year younger than myself, John Wesley—named after the founder of Methodism—and a daughter several years older. Her name was Dixie Dawn. Their conspicuous names seemed a part of their tragedy. John Wesley looked like his mother, which is to say he looked like a gorilla, with almost no forehead. The daughter was overweight and wore heavy makeup and had a pathetically angelic look about her. Although she was only thirteen she had large breasts. She sang in the Methodist church choir and said she wanted to sing soprano at the Met when she graduated from high school.

I was embarrassed by the family's appearance. In a way I

hated them for it, and yet I felt a certain sorrow as well and wished they had better things. Often I wondered how a person lives his life as part of such a family. I grieved for Dixie Dawn, and though she sang better than anyone I had ever known, I knew that she would get no closer to the Metropolitan Opera than a gas pump and a plate of cheese sandwiches at the end of a cotton row.

I rarely thought of the father at all, he was so seldom around.

And then one day as I was walking to the lot where I hoped to play baseball, I noticed that he was in the side yard working in the vegetable garden with a hoe. He was drunk and dirty, wearing baggy, unzipped trousers. His big belly was hanging out from under a sleeveless undershirt.

Dixie Dawn had come outside at the moment I was passing and had brought something to her father, something cool to drink.

Then for no apparent reason she stood there near him among the cabbages and began to sing. It was music of some operatic sort, some aria I suppose, clear and foreign and completely surprising.

This spontaneous music infuriated Mr. McNeer. He began cursing Dixie Dawn and berating her and calling her names. I was standing across the street watching. They did not see me, though it would not have mattered, he would have kept on in any case.

The abuse continued until Dixie Dawn was crying. Still it did not stop. Dixie Dawn was dressed in crisp seersucker, and though I hated her for her poverty and her fatness and her social ineptitude, she looked almost beautiful standing there among the cabbages and beans that her father had been hoeing.

Mr. McNeer's anger grew and grew, and the abuse became worse. Finally he walked towards her through the garden patch, and I was astonished to watch him strike Dixie Dawn over the head with the side of the hoe.

She staggered but did not fall. She turned to run. He followed and struck her many more times on the head and shoulders and back. He flung the hoe behind him and ran and caught her and stopped her. He was heavy and strong. He spun her around to face him and he held her by the shoulders. Her hair was black with blood. Her crisp dress was ruined. He shook her until she was as limp as a rag doll.

I could not hear his words, only the anger in his voice. Finally he let her go and she ran into the house, crying.

I hurried away from the scene, embarrassed and frightened. Before I was completely out of sight of them I turned and looked back and saw Dixie Dawn's mother coming out the door, calling angrily to her husband. I didn't wait to see more.

I hung around the vacant lot and waited for someone to show up to play ball. For a long time I was alone. I tossed the ball up in the air and caught it with my fielder's mitt. There was not much else to do. I thought of Dixie Dawn getting cracked over the head with the hoe. It was summer and the sun was beating down on the Delta. Fields of cotton plants stretched like long green carpets in all directions from where I stood. I could smell the cotton flowers on the wind. On the street a mule-drawn wagon trundled past, driven by a black man. The wagon was filled with blocks of ice and covered with a tarp. The ice melted and water poured out in streams beneath the wagon wheels.

At last another boy showed up, Roy Dale Conroy. Roy Dale was a white-trash child. He had milk-white skin and large coppery freckles. His hair was red and badly cut, probably by his older sister. He spat constantly, ptooey ptooey ptooey. It was a habit, a compulsion I would say.

Roy Dale was worthless as a playmate. He had no ball or glove or bat. He relied on the charity of others. He didn't really know how to play ball anyway. He would put the bat between his legs and make sexual jokes. Or he would put the ball down his pants and strut around. Nobody wanted to play with Roy Dale.

He said, "Hey, Sugar." Ptooey ptooey ptooey.

I said, "Hey, Roy Dale."

He said, "Throw me the ball. I want to show you something." Ptooey.

I said, "Mr. McNeer just beat Dixie Dawn over the head with a hoe."

Roy Dale went ptooey ptooey ptooey.

I said, "She was bleeding and everything."

He said, "Did she let you see her tits?"

I turned and headed for home. Roy Dale ran along and caught up with me.

He said, "Hey, man, just kidding. Take a joke."

I kept walking.

He said, "No kidding, let me see the ball. Just for a second. I'll give it right back."

We walked along towards my home. Roy Dale kept nagging me about the baseball.

I said, "She wants to sing opera songs."

He said, "I'll give you a quarter to let me see the ball."

We cut down an alley, a short way to my house. There was a weedy ditch with water running through it. Roy Dale said, "Hole up." He climbed down in the ditch and scrambled around, this way and that, grabbing at something in the weeds and finally cornering it in the water. He stepped in the ditchwater and didn't seem to notice that his shoes were wet. Finally he caught the thing he had been chasing, a mouse the size of a Ping-Pong ball.

We were in sight of my house now.

Roy Dale said, "What shall I do with it?" Talking about the mouse.

I said, "Let it go, Roy Dale."

He said, "I don't know. . . ." Teasing me.

I said, "Here, take it, take the ball." I held it out to him.

He said, "Hm. I don't really need the ball any more."

I said, "Don't hurt the mouse, Roy Dale. C'mon, take the ball."

He held the mouse tight in one hand. Its head stuck up between his fingers. It was tiny as a button, the little head, and yet all the features were distinct, the big ears and pointy face and little whiskers and frightened eyes like bright punctuation. It had little mouse-teeth, small as sand crystals.

Roy Dale took the baseball from me in his other hand.

He said, "I wonder which one I could throw farther."

I said, "You can have the ball. I'll give it to you. Let the mouse go. I'm telling you Dixie Dawn was bleeding all over the place. I thought he was going to kill her."

He said, "Do you mean it? I can have the ball?"

I said, "Just let the mouse go."

He said, "You're lying," and made me think he was about to hurl the mouse to the ground.

I said, "No, really. You can have it."

He said, "I don't want your fucking ball." He dropped the ball into the ditchwater and tossed the mouse underhand out in front of him in my direction. It was spinning in the air. I tried to catch the mouse but I missed it. It hit my hand and then my thigh and fell to the ground. The mouse was stunned but not badly injured. In a couple of seconds it got its bearings and scuttled off into the weeds.

Roy Dale picked the ball up out of the water and dried it against his pants and handed it to me. "Good as new," he said.

I said, "Thanks."

He said, "You might as well not lie to me about being your friend."

Roy Dale went his way and I went mine.

MY MOTHER was in the kitchen making homemade noodles and chicken broth. She hated noodles and broth, but it was the only thing my father would eat when he was drinking.

I walked into the kitchen and said, "Roy Dale caught a mouse and let it go."

She said, "To my mind a body needs a balanced diet."

I said, "Mr. McNeer hit Dixie Dawn over the head with a hoe and made her bleed."

Mama said, "Oh." She stopped what she was doing. She looked at me with sadness, her hands still covered with flour. I was glad I had told her.

I said, "She didn't do nothing. He just started beating her with the hoe."

She said, "Anything. She didn't do anything." And then she said, "Those poor sad people."

SOON AFTER the incident with the hoe Mrs. McNeer began a campaign to make her children's lives happy. She surprised local children on the street by giving them money. She would say, "My treat!" She volunteered to "help out" in the youth groups of every church in town. She made sandwiches for Methodist kids, she hired a truck for the Presbyterian hayride, she taught in the Baptist Vacation Bible School, she folk-danced with the Episcopalians.

Her unhappy children were always there with her. Dixie Dawn was forced to sing solos. John Wesley, who was tone deaf, stood around with his knuckles on the sidewalk.

Nothing worked, of course. Every child in town grew to fear and despise Dixie Dawn and John Wesley all the more.

The saddest event in the attempt to conscript an army against the McNeer children's misery was a birthday party for Dixie Dawn. I should say "birthday party," in quotation marks, since it was still summer and nobody's birthday at all. Dixie Dawn's birthday was not until February.

The party was elaborate. Maybe the most elaborate single event in white-trash history. Mrs. McNeer had prepared for forty or more children. She worked day and night for weeks. She strung crepe paper streamers from every available place, four separate colors of crinkly paper twisted together in a bright rope looping and swagging from house to store, from tree to bush. The yard was practically canopied in streamers.

Mrs. McNeer had rented a tent in case of rain, and had set it up and rolled up its sides and placed long cloth-covered tables beneath it. On the tables were foods that most of the children of Arrow Catcher, Mississippi, had never seen before.

Cucumber sandwiches cut with a cooky cutter, pickled her-
ring, olives, smoked oysters, raw vegetables with a mustard
dip, smoked bluefish and trout and salmon, even a liver pâté.
There were two large cakes. One of them said You're a Big Girl
Now. The other said Let's Boogie Down. There was a banner
that said Happy Birthday, and another that said Let's Have a
Party.

All across the lawn there were areas arranged for various
games. Card games here, board games there, blindfold games,
running games, croquet, badminton, every game you can
think of, all over the yard.

There were party favors beyond imagining. Honkers and
tooters and squeakers and clickers and tassled hats and sheriff's
badges and painter's caps and small magic tricks. Hand-
cuffs, fingercuffs, whoopee cushions, hand buzzers, squirting
flowers, leaky fountain pens, play money, sneezing powder,
itching powder, loaded dice, Mexican jumping beans, nose
flutes, nose putty, glow-in-the-dark teeth, riding crops. There
were Japanese lanterns and one million helium-filled balloons
on strings.

Most impressive of all was the ice cream. There was enough
ice cream for a hundred hungry people. It was homemade and
completely fresh. Fresh strawberry, fresh peach, fresh fig, I
don't know what else, but fresh, all of it fresh. Mrs. McNeer
lifted the freezing-cold lid of each metal canister, and the perfect cream pulled into a long smooth curl. The clop-clop of

hooves sounded in my mind as I imagined the ice wagon leaving off its entire load at the McNeer doorstep so that this perfection might be accomplished.

The problem with all this was that nobody came to the party.

I went to the party, no one else.


THE AFTERNOON was hot. We sat for a long time in new lawn chairs, me, Mrs. McNeer, Dixie Dawn (swollen with tears), and John Wesley, his hairline threatening to grow down over his eyes. All of us sat in the chairs and waited and waited for someone else to appear.

I could not even hate my parents for sending me here. I had not been sent. I came to this terrible place because I had to. I came because I had seen Mr. McNeer beat Dixie Dawn with the hoe. For that reason only. I was the only true guilty responsible witness to the sadness of their lives.

The minutes were hours, as we waited. Mrs. McNeer said, "No one wants to be first at a party." And she said, "Who said small-towners don't know how to be fashionably late?" And she said, "Where could all those other scamps be?" And she said, "All the expense . . ." And, "Their parents practically promised me."

No one came. The afternoon lengthened. The sun moved down the sky. Mrs. McNeer made a few futile phone calls. Finally there was nothing more to say.

One other person did come to the party. After a long while Roy Dale Conroy showed up. I am certain he had not been invited. He seemed only to happen past the house and to see us in the lawn chairs. He had been wading in a swamp and was wet to his knees and smelled like fish.

I had brought a small gift, a jar of hard candy wrapped in tissue paper. Roy Dale had brought no regular gift, of course, but he tried to give Dixie Dawn a quarter and a dime he found in his pocket.

Dixie Dawn refused to take the money, and then she refused to take the gift-wrapped package from me as well.

Mrs. McNeer insisted that she take the candy and then thank me for it. She ignored Roy Dale altogether.

Later Roy Dale offered the money to John Wesley, who took it and grinned like an ape and thanked him sincerely.

We played as many of the games as the five of us could play. We ate as much of the food as we could eat. We filled up bags of party favors to take home. Gallons of ice cream went to waste. We sang happy birthday to Dixie Dawn and she cried like the Missouri and went inside and lay down on her bed under an oscillating fan.

AND SO it was over. Or I thought so.

There was one more event on Mrs. McNeer's bizarre pathetic agenda. A campout, a sleep-over. Boys only. That was the way Mrs. McNeer put the proposition to us. Good news!

What fun! It's all decided, your parents have agreed. A pup tent! Have you ever heard of anything so wonderful, so fun! You can't escape, don't try. Everyone is invited.

WHAT CAN I say about my life that explains what it meant for me to lie hostage in a tent with these two companions?— Roy Dale and John Wesley. None of it is important. Only this day. The smell of gasoline at the pump, of souring cream, of defoliant and crisp leaves, a wagon pulling ice, noodles, broth, alcohol.

When night finally came, the party seemed to have been going on for centuries. Mrs. McNeer lighted a couple of lanterns in the backyard. She spread clean soft quilts on the bottom of the tent and laid out cheap sleeping bags on top of those. She opened up both ends of the tent so that we could catch a breeze, and dropped mosquito netting over the ends, just in case.

I forgave her for the lies she told to get us there. I doubted whether she had even bothered to lie to Roy Dale's parents. Probably he was there without permission, or for that matter without anyone's knowing or caring whether he came home that night.

We talked for a while in the tent, the three of us, John Wesley, Roy Dale, and me. Roy Dale said that he would teach us how to jack-off if we wanted him to. John Wesley said, "Oh boy! Yeah, sure, that would be great! Thanks!" But nothing ever came of the offer, and I was relieved.

We lay quiet for a while. We removed the mosquito netting and looked at the sky.

I said, "That's the North Star."

Roy Dale said, "You're lying."

He was right. I didn't know one star from another.

Roy Dale said, "I wish I had a cigarette."

It was a soft night. I was beginning to be glad I was there. I told Roy Dale and John Wesley the story of the day when I was five years old and a warning about a maddog went out through the neighborhoods. I made the memory sound dramatic. "No one was allowed on the streets," I said. "A maddog. A rabid dog." I told them that the air was filled with the fragrance of rotting persimmons and the sounds of wasps drunk on the ferment. This part was not true, I only told it to make the story sound better.

I thought Roy Dale would say, "You're lying."

Instead he said, "I remember that."

I said, "You do?"

He said, "I remember that maddog."

I said, "You're lying."

He said, "I saw it. It couldn't hardly walk, it was so crippled up with the disease."

I said, "Tell the truth."

He said, "There was ropes of spit stringing out of its mouth. Its eyes looked like busted marbles."

I said, "Oh, man."

He said, "A man with a rifle killed it. It was a shepherd dog. I saw a bright red bullet gash in its side. Mock it down: I watched that dog breathe its last breath."

We lay in the night silence and watched the stars. I wished I knew the names of all the stars and all the constellations. Or even just one of them.

I said, "Jeeziz."

Roy Dale still smelled like fish, but it was a good smell. The earth and its waters.

John Wesley spoke then. Soft little faraway ape-boy voice. He said, "The man who killed the dog was my daddy."

For a while there was only silence. For a while neither Roy Dale nor I even looked in his direction.

John Wesley was not lying. His father had been the man who killed the maddog and saved lives.

In a while Roy Dale was still, maybe he was asleep. I pretended to sleep as well, and then maybe I did fall asleep, and not long afterwards I woke up again and John Wesley was crawling out of the tent. John Wesley was barefoot, and wearing only his underwear.

He was headed towards the house.

I shook Roy Dale. I said, "Look."

John Wesley went inside the house through the back
screened door, and we saw him through the window, in the
kitchen with his sad mother beneath a lightbulb hanging from
a cord. They sat together at the kitchen table amidst the birthday wreckage, and though we could not have heard them in
any case, I think they did not speak.

And so we lay back in the tent, on our sleeping bags, and
did not speak either. We pretended to be asleep, though I was
not, and I am sure Roy Dale was not. After a while John
Wesley came back to the tent and crawled in between the two
of us and cried quietly until he slept, and so then sleep did
finally come to me, and then to Roy Dale, as well. The birthday party was over.

I SUPPOSE there is one more thing to tell. For many years,
after I was grown and no longer lived in Mississippi, I told this
story to my friends. And when I told it, I always added one
detail that was not true.

I always said that after we had settled down and had drifted
off to sleep beneath the canvas roof of the tent, I was awakened
in the middle of the night by the sound of Dixie Dawn's sweet
pure angelic voice in song. I said that beneath the bright stars
her voice was a crisp spirit, a lyrical hopeful pause in the
terrible drama of our narrow lives. I said—and even as I invented this I believed it—I said that in the foreign-language

music of her song my ears and my heart opened up to a world larger and more generous than the world of my parents and our geography.

Now as I tell this story again, I forget why I ever made up such a thing. It is not true, of course. Dixie Dawn did not wake up that night, so far as I knew. As far as I know, she lay in her bed in a hard deliberate sleep, where song had put her and from which song could never draw her out.

# A Hank of Hair, A Piece of Bone

THE SUMMER I turned eleven years old, I had a secret—it was a small collapsible military shovel, an entrenching tool, it was called.

I saw it in a junk store in Arrow Catcher, my little hometown in Mississippi, and something about the fold-up-and-tuck-away nature of the implement made it attractive to me. At the same time, I almost bought a metal canteen with a canvas cover—the metal dented and scratched, the canvas sun-faded and water-stained, ripe with authenticity. I envisioned filling it with Coca-Cola and, at night, secretly removing the cap and drinking lustily and privately in the dark. But when I unscrewed the lid and smelled inside, there was a hint of something that may have been urine, and so I passed on the canteen and paid my dollar for what was the real treasure anyway, the secret shovel.

There was no reason to hide the shovel; no one would have cared that I had it. And yet it was an instrument that begged to be hidden.

My bedroom was in the upstairs of my parents' home. It was small and interesting, with drawers and bookcases built into the walls to conserve space. In one wall there was also a desk, with pigeonholes and an inkwell, that could be revealed by unhooking a metal hook and dropping the desktop into place. There was a nice privacy in the hidden quality of the furniture in the walls.

And as long as I'm describing the room, I might as well tell that on the ceiling above my bed my mother had pasted luminous decals of stars and a moon and the planets—Saturn was prominent with its rings—and a comet with a tail. For a while after I turned off the lights at night, the little lunar system above me glowed with whatever sweet magic there is in such novelties. Outside my window the vastness of the Delta sky and its bright million stars and peach-basket-size moon could not compete with the galaxies inside my tiny bedroom and all its hidden geographies.

What I'm really getting at, though, is that in the back of my clothes closet—behind the hangers with trousers and shirts, behind the winter coats in plastic bags—there was a panel that could be removed to allow entrance into an even more secret spot, a crawlspace in the rafters.

On the day I bought the shovel, I removed the panel in the back of the closet and slipped inside the crawlspace to sit.

I had a stash of kitchen matches, from which I chose one and struck it and lighted a stub of a candle and then, careful not to set a fire, extinguished the match and spat on the tip. I sat cross-legged and sweaty in my hideout, inhaling the bad air of insulation and candle smoke, and thrilled at the invisibility of things.

And that was how I lived with my shovel for a while, I'm not sure how long, a couple of weeks I think.

Every day, when there was time, I crept into the crawlspace and found the wooden matches and lighted the candle stub and extended the collapsed handle of the shovel and heard the extension snap into place. And then, in the broiling Mississippi afternoon, or mornings if I woke up early enough, or sometimes at night when I should have been in my bed beneath the fake stars, my life was filled with the joy of secret things in secret places.

Soldier, miner, escaping prisoner—these were the games I played with the entrenching tool.

I had not yet used the shovel out-of-doors.


THE SUMMER inched through its humid hours. The figs on the trees along the chickenyard fence swelled up ("swole up," we said) and ripened and turned purple and fat. I played barefoot and barebacked in the shade of the broad fig leaves and sometimes picked the fruit from the limbs and watched the ooze of fig-milk from the stem as it covered my fingers. The figs were like soft wood on my tongue, and a sweet residue of poison hung in the Delta air, where the ditches had been sprayed for mosquitoes.

Some days my father brought home a watermelon, green-striped and big as a washtub, and the three of us, mother, father, and myself, cut it beneath the walnut tree and ate big seedy red wedges of melon in the metal lawnchairs.

Evenings my father fed the chickens—the Plymouth Rocks, the Rhode Island Reds, slow and fat and powdered with dust—and my mother made fig preserves and sealed the syrupy fruit in Mason jars with hot paraffin lids.

It is tempting to look back at this time and to remember only those images of ripeness and joy.

Many evenings my father was drinking whiskey. He never drank before he was bathed and clean at the end of a day's work—he smelled of Lifebuoy soap and Fitch's shampoo and Wildroot Cream Oil, and of course of the Four Roses bourbon, masculine and sweet as wooden barrels.

Sometimes my parents fought their strange fight. The day I am remembering was a Friday.

The three of us were in the kitchen. My mother said to my father, "I wish you wouldn't do that, Gilbert."

I was standing in front of the refrigerator with the door open, looking for nothing in particular.

My father was at the sink with the water running. He held a tall water glass beneath the spigot and allowed it to fill up, and then he poured the glass of water into the sink. He filled the glass again, and then poured it into the sink again. And as the water ran from the tap, he filled the glass and poured out its contents, over and over, glass after glass, maybe twenty times without speaking.

My mother could only say, "I wish you wouldn't do that, Gilbert," as she watched him, silent and withdrawn, filling and pouring, filling and pouring at the sink.

I closed the refrigerator door and watched my father pour out one final glass of water. Then he stopped. This was a thing he did every day, and it gave my mother distress. When he was finished, he did as always—he placed the glass on the sink and stood for a while longer and watched the water run from the pipe into the drain. Then slowly, deliberately, he turned the handle and shut off the flow.

That was the end of it. After the water-pouring episode, my father went to his room and closed the door and my mother went into her own room—she called it a guest bedroom, but it was her own, with her underwear in the drawers, her bobby pins on the dresser—and lay across her bed and cried.

I could hear her from the kitchen, and I could hear music from my father's phonograph, and I knew that he was drinking from a bottle hidden in his chest-of-drawers and that he would not come out until morning.

I wanted to comfort my mother, but there was nothing to say. I stood by the kitchen sink and looked at the glass my father had been filling and emptying, and I believed for the one-millionth time that if I looked at it long enough, tried hard enough, I could understand what my parents' strange fighting meant.

Tonight I went to my father's room, a thing I ordinarily never did after they fought, or after he closed the door and started to drink in earnest.

I knocked at his door and waited. I knew he would not answer and he did not. I knocked again and said, "Daddy," and waited again.

I heard movement inside his room, his chair, I supposed—a green-painted metal lawnchair, which he used as an easy chair—scraping against the hardwood floor. The chair sat on a rounded frame, which allowed it to rock back and forth.

After a silence the door opened and I could tell that my father was already very drunk. He looked at me and finally moved aside to let me in. He sat in his strange lawnchair and his record kept playing softly on the phonograph, a slow ballad sung by Elvis. The whiskey bottle was not in sight.

He said, "What is it, Sugar?"

My father was not a tall man, no more than five feet six inches, and his childlike shoes, with crepe soles and shiny uppers, were covered with tiny speckles of paint. His feet did not reach the floor except as the chair rocked forward. He was wearing Big Smith khakis and an open-necked shirt, and I noticed that the face of his watch was flecked with paint.

I said, "I bought a shovel." I had not known I was going to say this.

My father let a few seconds pass and then he said, "Is that right."

I said, "I've got it in my room."

He said, "Do you want a peppermint puff?" My father reached across the top of the phonograph to a cellophane bag filled with peppermint candy and brought out a small handful and put one piece of candy into his mouth. I held out my hand and received a piece.

I said, "I haven't dug anything with it yet." I put the candy in my mouth, the peppermint puff, and it was light and airy as magic. It seemed almost to float instead of melt inside my mouth.

And then, as unexpectedly as I had announced the existence of the shovel, my father said, "The Delta is filled up with death."

Now that I look back on this moment I think that he meant nothing at all by this remark. Probably the mention of a shovel made him think of graves and that made him think of death, which was his favorite drunken subject anyway. Self-pity, self-dramatization—the boring death-haunted thoughts of an alcoholic, nothing more.

And yet, at the time, the words he spoke seemed directly related to my accidental, unintentional mention of the shovel, the way advice is related to a problem that needs to be solved.

I said, "It is?"

He said, "Yep. To the brim."

The conversation was over. I stayed a little longer, but already my father was growing irritable and restless, and I knew he wished I would leave so that he could drink from the bottle in the chest-of-drawers.

THE DELTA was filled with death. The information came like a summons, a moral imperative to search.

And so that day, and for many days afterwards, I took the shovel outside and started to dig. In the front yard the shovel blade cut through the grass and scarred the lawn. I replaced the squares of sod before my mother could see the damage, but already I knew I was doing the right thing. Earthworms retreated to cooler, safer depths. Roly-polies curled up into little balls. The blade of the shovel shone at the edges, the dirt was fragrant and cool to my touch.

My first serious digging was a trench alongside the back of the chickenyard, near the fence. The earth there was loamy and soft and worm-rich and easy to dig. I threw spadefuls of loose dirt at the busy old hens and watched them scatter and puff out their feathers as large as beach balls.

What was I digging for? Indians had lived on this land, Chickasaws and Choctaws. Slaves had died here. There might be bones. A well-digger once dug up a Confederate mortar shell near the dog pen and it was still on display in the Plantation Museum in Leflore. Sometimes a kid would find an arrowhead or spear point. My father was right—the remains of other civilizations did still occasionally poke through into our own.

So there was a sense in which I was only following my father's advice—I was digging for evidence of other worlds. And for a while the hard work of digging, and the work of hiding its consequences, were enough.

The trench by the fence was a mistake. A neighborhood dog crawled under and killed my father's blue Andalusian rooster, and I had to fill the trench and get the dog out before anyone could figure out that I was responsible. I threw the dead rooster into some tall weeds near the trailer where the midgets lived, and so my father thought it had flown the coop and been killed as a result of its own restlessness and vanity. So that was good.

I kept on digging. All the holes I dug were in some way unsatisfactory.

Beneath the walnut tree the earth was rock-hard and root-congested, and I was afraid of breaking the shovel handle.

The last of several holes I dug on the lake bank, which was softer ground, finally yielded a few bones, but they were in a plastic garbage bag and, though it took me a while, I finally understood that they were the skeleton of a big tom cat that belonged to a neighbor-woman, Mavis Mitchum. The cat had been hit by a car last winter.

Along the ditch at the back of the house I dug up a nest of ground-hornets and was stung seven times. I dug each day and found a good deal of unpleasantness but little death in the Delta.

I have to ask the question again: What was I digging for?—skeletons?—Indians? Not really, not at first, though I thought of those things in a general way. I think I was only playing, only digging for fun. I was a child, and I enjoyed the child's play, as I had enjoyed the games behind my closet, in the crawlspace.

And yet the more I dug—the greater number of holes I emptied and refilled, the more often I heard the shovel blade cut the soil and breathed the mold-and-mulch-rich fragrance of overturned earth and felt its heft in my hands, and watched the retreat of the earthworms and the vivid attack of the hornets and the other evidences of life beneath the surface of the earth—mole tunnels and rabbit holes—the more I feared and was driven to discover evidence of death.

And so by some process I became not the soldier or prisoner I had pretended to be in the crawlspace, not a child with a game, but a person driven by some need born of my father's pain, my mother's despair.

My occupation became not only more necessary but more real, more dark in character. I was no longer pretending to be a soldier or prisoner, but now, without the protection of fantasy at all, I was a real-life gravedigger, possessed and compulsive—and not merely a gravedigger but a hopeful graverobber, a sad

innocent little ghoul spading my way through the Delta, looking for God knows what, some signal or symbol, I don't know,
whatever a child in need and fear is capable of looking for after
talking to his drunken father about a shovel.

I don't blame my father. What would be the point? There is
a sense in which I blame the geography itself, though that, of
course, is useless as well.

The more I dug in the Delta earth, the more it seemed to
call me to dig, the more certain I became that it would finally
yield up some evil treasure.

I turned over spadeful after spadeful. I dug all over our
small property—back yard and front yard and chicken yard. I
dug out by Roebuck Lake, and even in Mavis Mitchum's yard,
the neighbor-woman. Some of the holes were deep, some were
long shallow trenches. I looked in each spadeful of earth for
some sign—a toe, a tooth, some small thing, a knuckle.
There was nothing.

I moved underneath the house—Delta houses have no base-
ments—and here beneath the floorboards and waterpipes, in
the slick, sun-untouched hard-packed earth, my digging took
new meaning. No longer frantic, no longer directionless, my
entire body slowed down, the way a body is slowed down by
age. I was a strong child—thin but sturdy—and I had the will
to dig, the iron will of a child's burden of his parents' unhap-
piness. I would dig to China if necessary. I was digging a hole

beneath my house, and I knew I would find whatever I had been looking for.

THE UNDERSIDE of the house was a different world to me. Suddenly plumbing made sense—pipes going in and coming out. The light was filtered and cool. The dirt was slick and ungrassed for half a century. The outside world, glimpses of it, was allowed into my vision only through chinks in the brick foundation. Above me were the boards of the floor where my parents walked. Refuse had been thrown under here, a slick tire, a bald baby-doll, a wooden case of Coke bottles, an ice pick my daddy had once stabbed himself in the chest with. The house was an old structure, sixty or seventy years old, and other families had lived here before my own. Even in the refuse—the broken glass, a dog-food can, two cane poles—there was a sense that lives had been lived here, that death had defeated them.

I kept on digging. I could not stand up to dig—the floor was directly above me—so I lay on my side. I stabbed the blade into the earth and, with the strength of my arms, lifted out the dirt. The work was slow and laborious. Spadeful after spadeful, I dragged dirt out of the hole and piled it away from me in a mound.

Each day I was tired and filthy, the muscles of my arms were hot with strain. I worried that my mother would stop me from what I was doing.

She did not. She only knew that I was playing under the house. She warned me about broken bottles, she grouched at me about the dirt in my jeans. But our lives went on. I continued to dig.

There were happy days, with watermelon, and sad days of whiskey. The hole beneath the house grew deeper and wider, and the mound beside the hole grew taller. My father continued to pour glasses of water down the sink, my mother begged him not to. "I wish you wouldn't do that, Gilbert." I had a sense of doing something worthwhile, or at least necessary in the face of the many things I could not otherwise control.

I kept on, possessed I would say, and sometimes fear of what I was looking for would overtake me. I would sit beside the hole and cry—*weep* is a better word, since there was as much drama in this as there was sadness—and often I would wish that I had never heard of this hole, that I had never bought this shovel, that I had bought the wicked canteen instead.

I was afraid that whatever I found—joint, knuckle, or tooth—would be too personal to endure. Suddenly, or rather gradually, this became no abstraction I was searching for, not merely *death*. I believed now that whatever bone I found—and I had no doubt I would find something, however small—was not without a human history, that a single bone was a person, someone whose life was as filled with madness and loss as the lives of my father and mother.

I believed I could not endure knowing more about such sadness than I already suspected. My throat ached. I imagined that whatever relic I found would contain within it the power to reconstruct an entire self, a finger joint becoming a hand, the hand recreating an arm, the arm a torso, with chest hair and a head and knees. Dry bones becoming meat and, immediately, the meat reclaiming the right and capacity to rot and fall away, and bones to be scattered and lost.

So I continued to dig underneath the house. I dug long past the time when I enjoyed it. It was a job to me, this digging, it was medicine necessary in some way to my continued life, neither joyful nor joyless, a thing to be done, a hole to be dug.

The underside of my house became as familiar to me as the crawlspace behind my closet. I stopped digging sometimes and lay on my back beneath the house, beside the hole, which now was deep—two feet deep and two feet wide, and then wider and deeper. I dug down to three feet, and the hole was squared off, like the grave of a child. I kept on digging. I lay in exhaustion, down in the hole, and looked up at the floorboards of the house. I heard my mother's footsteps above me in the kitchen. I heard the boards make their small complaint. Water ran through the pipes around me—surging up through pipes into the house and into the sink, or going the other way, out of the house through the larger pipes, down into the earth and away.

I lay in the dirt and looked at the floorboards, as sweat

drained out of me, my back and arms, and soaked down into the same earth. I imagined that my sweat flowed under the earth like a salty river, that it entered the water table and into a seepage of sand grains and clay and, from there, into Roebuck Lake, its dark still waters. Around me sunlight broke through the cracks in the foundation in points as brilliant as diamonds, and underneath my house was always twilight, never day and never dark.

ONE DAY in my digging—who can remember which day, a Thursday, a Saturday?—all the summer days were the same— my shovel struck something and my heart stopped, seemed to stop, tried to stop. I had found whatever I had been destined to find. Directed to find: by the man at the junk store, by the canteen, which had whispered *take the shovel not me,* by my father at the sink. My shovel struck something—hard, solid, long, like a sheet of heavy glass, a table top—and my heart, stopped dead by fear and awe, cried out for this to be some innocent thing, a pirate's chest, a sewer line.

I took only one look, and never looked again, and so what I tell you is only what I saw, not what I know to have been there. I was lying in the hole I had dug, this grave, its dark dirt walls on four sides of me. I was comfortable with my entrenching tool. I touched the earth again with the shovel, and again heard the noise of its blade against a sheet of heavy glass.

I thought, in that moment before I brushed away the dirt

and took one brief look through a glass window into the past, or into my own troubled heart, whichever it really was, of a nursery rhyme my mother had said to me many times at night, beneath the fake stars.

It was the tale of a woman who goes to the fair and falls asleep beneath a tree and, while she sleeps, has the hem of her petticoat cut off and stolen by a thief. Without her petticoat she doesn't recognize herself when she wakes up, and she wonders who this strange woman with no petticoat can be. Even when she gets home and looks in the mirror, she is unfamiliar to herself. She says, "Dearie dearie me, is it really I?"

I could not believe that I was the person with this shovel, on this brink.

I brushed the dirt off the sheet of glass and allowed my eyes their one second of looking. Beneath the glass was a dead woman, beautiful, with auburn hair and fair skin. Her head was resting on a blanket of striped ticking.

One second, less than a second, and I never looked again. I averted my eyes and put down the shovel and crawled up out of the hole. Without looking down into the hole again, I filled the hole with the dirt I had taken out. I pushed it with my hands until it spilled over the sides of the grave and covered the shovel and whatever else was there or not there.

The dress she was wearing was red velvet, down to her ankles. Her shoes were tiny, with pointed toes. The slipper was leather and the boot was of some fabric, silk I thought. On one finger was a gold ring in the shape of a bent spoon.

It is impossible that I saw all this in one glance—her whole length, her tiny feet and fingers. It is impossible that I brushed away a bit of dirt and saw her entirely, her fingers, her hair, an exposed calf that showed the fabric of her boot.

And yet I know that I did see this, and that one second later I covered it up and did not look again.

I sat there in the dirt, beneath the floorboards of my parents' home, and I saw another thing, a gaggle of white geese being chased by a fox, but I knew even then that these were not real geese but only the erratic beating of my heart made visible. The woman in the glass coffin?—still I am not sure what was real and what my mind invented.

The sound of my parents' footsteps was above me, where I sat in the twilight of this cloistered world. In the dead woman's face I had seen my mother's beauty, the warm blood of her passion, as my father had once known her and had forgotten. I heard water running in the sink above me and imagined, whether it was true or not, that it was my father filling and emptying tumblers of water, and all around me I heard this poured-out water gurgling down through pipes, headed for sewers, the water table, the gills of gars in Roebuck Lake. Through the floorboards I could hear voices, the sound not the words, and I believed it was my mother's voice begging my father not to pour his life down this sad drain, glass after glass, day after day, until she too was empty of life and hope.

I kept sitting there, thinking of the dead woman, and I imagined her in a church pew with a songbook on her lap. I imagined her on a riverboat (if she was real she might have died a hundred years before and been buried here, pickled, perfectly preserved in alcohol or some other fluid, mightn't she?— could she not have died on one of the riverboats that once floated from the Yazoo into the Roebuck harbor?), on the deck of a boat and holding a yellow parasol. I imagined her in a green back yard, hanging out sheets on a line. I saw her eat cantaloupe and spit out the seeds, secret and pretty, into a bed of bright flowers. I saw her leading a horse by a blue bridle from an unpainted barn.

I named her pretty names. Kate and Molly and Celia, even Leda, and I called her none of these names for fear of changing something too fragile ever to be named, the same reason I did not look at her longer, for fear she could not exist in the strength of more than a second's looking. In my mind, as I named her, my father's name kept ringing, over and over, with a sound like wooden ducks in a carnival shooting gallery when they are knocked over, the ding and ding and ding, and the slap of their collapse.

I left the underside of the house and never went back.

I went inside and surprised my mother by bathing and

washing my hair with Fitch's shampoo in the middle of the afternoon, and without being told. I put my dirty clothes into the washer and set the dial, and while the machine made them clean, I dressed in fresh blue jeans and a button-up shirt and dug the dirt out from under my fingernails and cleaned the mud off my shoes.

In my mind I gave the woman gifts. I gave her a candle stub. I gave her a box of wooden kitchen matches. I gave her a cake of Lifebuoy soap. I gave her a ceilingful of glow-in-the-dark planets. I gave her a bald baby doll. I gave her a ripe fig, sweet as new wood, and a milkdrop from its stem. I gave her a peppermint puff. I gave her a bouquet of four roses. I gave her fat earthworms for her grave. I gave her a fish from Roebuck Lake, a vial of my sweat for it to swim in.

I combed my hair with Wildroot Cream Oil and ate an entire package of my father's peppermint candy and puked in the toilet.

My mother said, "Sugar, are you all right?"

I said, "You bet," and walked boldly into my father's room and stole two rubbers from a box of Trojans in the drawer of his bedside table, and as long as I had the drawer open, took out his pistol and spun the cylinder and aimed it at the green lawn rocker and cocked the hammer with my thumb and then eased it back down. I stole two bullets from a box of cartridges in the drawer.

Later I walked beside Roebuck Lake and threw away the rubbers and the bullets and hated my father and myself.

THE SUMMER was long and its days were all the same. The poison in the ditches was sweet, the mosquitoes were as loud as violins, as large as owls. The cotton fields smelled of defoliant, and the cottonstalks were skeletons in white dresses. As summer deepened, the rain stopped, and so the irrigation pumps ran night and day in the rice paddies. My father took my mother dancing at the American Legion Hut, and I went with them and put a handful of nickels in the slot machine near the bar and won enough money to keep on playing for hours.

The black man behind the bar—his name was Al, and he drove an Oldsmobile—took me to the piano and showed me an eight-beat measure with his left hand and said it was the boogie-woogie beat and if I listened right I could hear it behind every song ever written, every song that for a lifetime would ever make my toes feel like tap-tap-tapping.

That night it was true, and I still listen for it. I could hear it, this under-music, like a heartbeat, in the tunes my parents were dancing to. I could hear it in the irrigation pumps in the rice paddies. I could hear it in the voice of the preacher at the Baptist church, and in the voice of a carny who barked at the freak show. I heard it in the stories my mother told me at night. I heard it in the tractors in the fields and in the remembered music of my shovel, my entrenching tool, its blade cutting into the earth, and in the swarm of hornets, and in the bray of mules, and in the silence of earthworms.

I watched my father and mother dance in the dim light of the dance floor, the only two dancers that night, and I fell in love with both of them, their despair and their fear and also their strange destructive love for each other and for some music I was growing old enough to hear, that I heard every day in the memory of the woman in her private grave. My father was Fred Astaire, he was so graceful, and my mother—though before this night I had seen her only as a creature in a frayed bathrobe standing in the unholy light of my father's drinking— she was an angel on the dance floor. The simple cotton dress that she wore was flowing silk—or was it red velvet?— and her sensible shoes were pointy-toed leather slippers with a silk boot. I understood why the two of them had been attracted to each other. I understood, seeing them, why they continued in their mutual misery. Who can say it was not true love, no matter how terrible?

In this dim barnlike room—the felt-covered poker tables, the dark bright wood of the dance floor, the upright piano, a lighted Miller's sign turning slowly on the ceiling, a nickel slot by the bar—here I loved my parents and the Mississippi Delta, its poisoned air and rich fields, its sloughs and loblollies and coonhounds and soybeans. In everything, especially in the whisk-whisk-whisk of my parents' feet on the sawdusty dance floor, I heard the sound of the boogie-woogie beat, eight notes—five up the scale and three down—I heard it in the clash and clatter of the great machines in the compress, where loose cotton, light as air, was smashed into heavy bales and wrapped in burlap and tied with steel bands. I held onto my secret, the dead woman under our house, and wished that I could have known these things about my parents and our geography and its music without first having looked into the dead woman's face and held inside me her terrible secret.

My father and mother danced and danced, they twirled, their bodies swayed to the music, their eyes for each other were bright. My father sang to my mother an old tune, sentimental and frightening, crooning his strange love to her, *oh honeycomb won't you be my baby oh honeycomb be my own,* he sang, this small man enormous in his grace, *a hank of hair and a piece of bone my honeycomb.* My mother placed her head on his shoulder as they danced, and when she lifted her face he kissed her lips and they did not stop dancing.

THERE IS one more thing to tell.

Late in the summer, deep in August, when the swamps were steam baths, and beavers as big as collies could be seen swimming in Roebuck Lake from a canebrake to a willow shade, I passed my eleventh birthday.

I still had told no one about the corpse, if it was a corpse and not something equally terrifying, a vision or hallucination born of heartbreak and loss, beneath our house. The shovel was a forgotten toy.

My mother made me a birthday cake in the shape of a rabbit—she had a cake pan molded in that shape—and she decorated it with chocolate icing and stuck on carrot slices for the eyes. It was a difficult cake to make stand up straight, but with various props it would balance on its hind legs on the plate, so that when I came into the room it looked almost real standing there, its little front feet tucked up to its chest.

At the sight of the rabbit I started to cry. My mother was startled by my tears. She had been standing in the doorway between the kitchen and the dining room. The table was set with a white tablecloth and linen napkins, three settings for my birthday dinner.

I could not stop crying, looking at that rabbit cake. I knew that my mother loved me, I knew something of her grief— something in the desperate innocence of the rabbit, its little yellow carrot eyes. I thought of the hopelessness of all love, and that is why I was crying, I think.

My mother came to me and held me to her and I felt her warmth and smelled her woman-smell. I wanted to dance with her at the Legion Hut. I wanted to give her a gift of earthworms.

I kept crying.

My mother said, "Oh, Sugar-man . . ."

I kept on crying, sobbing, trying to talk between the sobs. I said, "There's a woman under the house."

She said, "I know, Sugar-man, I know, hush now . . ."

I said, "I don't want to listen to the boogie-woogie beat."

She said, "I know, darling, I know . . ."

She kept on holding me, rocking me where we stood.

I said, "It's a dead woman. Under our house."

She said, "I know, Sugar-man, I know . . ."

I said, "In a grave."

She said, "I know, darling, you hush now . . ."

I said, "I don't want my toes to go tap-tap-tapping."

# Train, Train, Coming
# round the Bend

W H E N I was a child of eleven, there was a snail-slow freight train of a dozen cars or less that dragged its back legs through town each morning like a sorry dog and even stopped momentarily for God knows what reason at the Arrow Catcher depot and rested itself long enough to catch its breath and then, as if hopelessly, gathered its strength once again and set out on its asthmatic straining greasy little diesel motion towards the Mississippi River, some forty miles west of where I lived.

This was the summer a man was executed in Greenville. And it was the year my grandfather lived with us—my blind, bitter grandfather, I need to say—and listened to St. Louis Cardinals baseball on a Philco radio as big as the Frigidaire.

One day that summer, after a night when the Delta had been washed by a jungle rain, I hid in the ditch down by the track where I knew the last freight car would rest when the train made its daily stop, and I waited until the chuffy little sorry excuse for a train came to a stop and I pulled myself up the ditch bank by holding clumps of grass and wiped my hands on my pants and grabbed the ladder of a boxcar and swung myself up onto its first rung and held myself there as the train creaked forward out of the station.

I only rode through town, hanging onto the ladder, past the

Old Dixie Cafe, past Mr. Wooten's Shoe Shop, which stood on a block of stores with a wooden sidewalk, past the Quong Chong Fancy Gro., and the Kingfisher Market. The train got scarcely above five miles an hour, and if I had at any point let go of the ladder and dropped to the ground, I could have easily outrun the train to the apple orchard two hundred yards down the track, where I could have jumped clear and walked back home as the slimy little worm of a diesel and its spineless freight cars continued with threats of speed down the Delta flatscape towards the river.

I did this a half dozen times that summer. And then one day, for what reason I cannot say, something changed. I hooked the train, as I had done before. The Delta was what it had always been—endless blue sky, defoliated fields, small African villages peopled with princes and savages and their barebreasted sad women, washpots and collard greens. The train was what it had always been, so slow, so comfortable that it seemed to be stasis in motion. The poison heat of the diesel exhaust which swept back into my face was no different from the normal usual poisonous air that blew across the Mowdown in the paddies or the DDT in the ditches and made up the staple air of my comfort and ease. Everything was the same. The train wagged its reluctant head and heaved itself up like an old man and set out with a wonted resignation toward the orchard where I usually jumped clear. Bark from the pulpwood on a flatcar was blowing in my face when I realized that I was not going to jump off.

I didn't jump. The apples on the trees called me to jump, but I did not. The train kept on, down the track, slow as a cow. My body relaxed. I held on easily. I leaned out from the boxcar and looked ahead, down the track. The apple trees crept back behind me, their voices did not reach my ears, which were filled only with the bad-lung sounds of the train, which suddenly caused me to laugh like a happy person.

I rode the train out of town. Someone might as well have been ringing Christmas bells inside my body, my insides were so alive with anxiety and joy.

The train eased into a bend and along a length of Panther Burn, a snaky stream with brakes of bamboo along the banks. It did not increase in speed, it only moved along the track.

I saw a dead dog alongside the railroad track and knew that this animal had committed suicide, there was no other explanation for how it could have been struck by this train. Farther along, a flock of red-wing blackbirds stood pecking at something in the gravel one foot away from the track. I could have jumped into the middle of them, they were so unaffected by our comical huffing and commotion.

I saw roadhouses I had never seen before, Leonard's and Paradise Inn. I saw a woman beating a child. I saw an old man clogging on a bridge. I saw a horse with a blue bridle. I saw a jeep stuck in a field. I saw a yellow cat with a sparrow in its mouth. I saw lespedeza and wisteria. I saw cowbirds on a barbed wire fence. I saw empty wine bottles in the roadbed. My eyes could now suddenly see long distances.

The train kept on down the track. It even gained a little speed. It rocked like a dangerous cradle. I climbed up the ladder to the top of the boxcar. I stood and spraddled my legs and let the train rock on. The train's motion was my own motion. I walked a few steps along the moving car. At first I was stiff-legged and cautious and then I walked with confidence. I danced a country-boy jig. I laughed my damn head off. Git on down the road!

The train slowed then, five miles outside of Arrow Catcher, and then it stopped at a little gray building, a tiny depot, with the word QUITO spelled out on its sign. The tired old train knelt down with its tongue hanging out and heaved deep breaths and nursed a stitch in its side. Whoo, shit! the little train seemed to say, a little too pleased with itself for its brief speed, as I scooted back down the ladder and headed out walking, back down the track five miles to my home in Arrow Catcher. Walking, walking, don't give a flip!

NO ONE had missed me, of course. And when they saw me no one noticed that I had been transformed by imagination and the possibility of distances.

The danger of what I had just done was small—a fall from a

height of a few feet at walking speed was less dangerous than a dozen risks I took every day of the summer. Often, with other boys my age, I jumped from the Roebuck trestle into a few feet of water to test how far I could stick myself into the mud of the lake bottom. One boy actually hit a submerged boat and broke his back, and yet we jumped. But for all its benign aspect, my illicit ride on the Southern was not a secret I was likely to share with either my father or my mother. The danger of being chopped up by the wheels was meaningless. I was afraid my parents would understand the real danger, the great magnetism, the centrifugal pull away from everything familiar and true.

I WOULD not tell my parents, but I considered telling my blind grandfather, who despised me. It was a Saturday afternoon and the sun shafts through the window of his room were as solid as pine planks. The Delta was a steam bath, and my grandfather's space heater was roaring like a log fire. My grandfather was dressed up, as always, in a suit and vest and silk ascot and a watch and fob chain as heavy as leg irons and sweating in the impossible heat like a man on death row. My grandfather believed he might sweat the blindness out of his system. The dark glasses that he wore to cover his affliction kept slipping down his oiled nose and he had to push them up again with his forefinger.

As I came into my grandfather's room the hypnotist was just

giving up. My grandfather paid him, and he scurried away with big wet spots underneath the arms of his shirt.

Grandfather said, "He was more useless than the faith healer."

I said, "I rode on the freight train."

He said, "Musial just batted. You missed it." He was listening on the big Philco, which partly explained the hypnotist's failure.

I said, "I jumped off at Quito station."

He said, "Tripled off the right field fence, but you missed it. You always miss it."

I said, "I danced on a boxcar."

He said, "Will dancing cure blindness?"

I said, "It might."

He said, "Go git me a Co-Cola."

I said, "What time is it?"

He pulled out his watch and checked it. He said, "I don't know. I'm blind."

I said, "The equator is a railroad track."

He said, "Go git me that Co-Cola. Acupuncture don't work. Surgery don't work. Power of positive thinking don't work."

I said, "Can I have a drink out of it?"

He said, "Voodoo don't work. Ophthalmology sure as hell don't work."

I brought him a Coca-Cola and took a big swig before I handed it to him.

He said, "You slobbered all over it."

I said, "Slobber might work."

He said, "Don't nothing work. Won't nothing cure blindness."

I said, "Where does the train go when it leaves Quito station?"

He said, "Hush. Musial is about to bat."

I said, "He just batted."

He said, "Hush. He's on deck. Stan the Man is in the batter's circle."

My failure as a baseball fan was a cause of my grandfather's blindness and isolation. Musial batted every time I walked into the room.

NOT THIS night but a night in the same summer, my family sat eating together, my mother's nightmarish cooking before us. With the proper tools a patio could have been built from my mother's rice. The only thing that could penetrate it was her acid gravy, in which now soaked some substance in the shape of meat. The table was covered with a sheet of something we called oilcloth, and when my mother warned against spilling gravy on it, I took her warning seriously, having once heard the words *chemical reaction*.

It was August, and whatever it was that governed my solitude—rage, I think now—was disguised as comfort. For weeks I had ridden the train across town. More often I only put my ear to the steel rail and listened to the solitary music as the train rolled onto the Runnymeade trestle. Once I put a penny on the track and let the train roll over it. When I found it again, the coin was a wafer the size and color of a perfectly cooked pancake. Abraham Lincoln was as unfamiliar as a midget in the sideshow.

And now, just hours before this bad meal, Portable Justice had arrived in Arrow Catcher in a van that looked like the Bookmobile.

The electric chair was part of an exhibit sponsored by the State of Mississippi and hauled around to eighty-two county seats. It was happening, the State was telling us. The execution was real. A man would die in this incredible chair before Labor Day, and Mississippians were invited to lay eyes upon the instrument of his destruction.

I stood in the air-conditioned van with other children and adults and looked at the chair. The van was brightly lighted. There were framed pictures on the walls—the president, the governor. Even a framed news clipping of the first man ever put to death by electrocution, a *New York Times* article dated April 28, 1898. The man's name was there, and even his picture, with a starched collar and a silly smile.

The chair itself was as big as a roadside fruit stand. It was hardly a chair at all, a horrible throne. It was made of oak timbers, it had a seat wide enough for three condemned men, arms wide enough to rest a dinner plate on. There were two heavy-duty wires. One went to a steel beanie for the head, the other went to a steel cuff for the right calf. There were heavy leather straps that seemed darkened with sweat. Two straps came down from the top of the chair to hold the condemned man by the shoulders. There were straps for the wrists and the ankles and even a strap for the forehead. There was a heavy leather strap a foot wide that went across the condemned man's waist. One of several high school boys looking at the exhibit said, "Buckle up for safety," and the others snickered.

The exhibit guide was a thin man with a narrow nose and thin lips. He gave the high school boys an evil look. He seemed to say, "You go on acting like that and it could be you sitting in that chair some day." I agreed with the look. I was silent and respectful.

The guide said, "The condemned man may choose anything he wishes for his last meal." I thought, If he chose my mother's rice, he wouldn't need to waste the electricity. I thought I would choose steak and french fries. Or maybe I would just ask for suggestions.

The guide said, "The top of the head is shaved." He said, "The right calf is also shaved." The high school boys said, "Woo-woo," and pretended that sounded sexy. The weasely guide gave them another look and they shut up. The guide said, "A salt solution is applied to the shaved areas to insure perfect contact."

Suddenly I said, "Can I sit in it?"

The guide looked at me. He said, "Suit yourself," and stood aside to allow me to sit down.

I looked back at the high school boys, who suddenly seemed quiet and afraid. I sat in the chair. Then I heard one of them say, "You're sitting where many a grinning nigger died."

It was this same night that I was sitting at my parents' table.

My mother said, "More rice and gravy?" Speaking to my father.

My father said, "Well, you bet." My father loved my mother's incredible cooking.

I said, "I don't want none, Mama."

My grandfather said, "Sugar don't know what's good. You go blind, you'll appreciate good food." He said, "I'm hungry, I'm so hungry I can't see straight."

My mother said, "Hand me your plate, Pap. Some rice and gravy might help."

I said, "I'm taking the freight train to the execution."

My grandfather said, "Won't nothing help. Won't nothing cure blindness of the eyes."

I said, "Mock it down. I'm taking the freight train to see a man get the shock of his life."

My father said, "They's a blue smoke coming off this gravy."

My mother said, "Spoon some over a slice of that Wonder Bread, you want a special treat."

My grandfather said, "I don't even remember the color blue, I been blind so long."

I said, "It's the color of sparks flying out of your nose when they pull the switch."

My grandfather spooned the chemical fluid straight out of the gravy boat and into his mouth to break up a rice blockage in his throat. He said, "Getting rid of you might help."

He said this beneath his breath, but he was fierce and serious and I heard him.

My mother said, "Now, Pap."

My grandfather said, "Eleven years old and still don't know how to listen to the radio."

I said, "Can I watch television?"

My father said, "I don't want you watching any colored people on that television."

My grandfather said, "Sammy Davis is on tonight. I heard about it."

My father said, "Better leave the TV alone tonight, Sugar."

My grandfather said, "If he knew how to listen to the radio he wouldn't have to watch a bunch of coons on the TV."

My mother, said, "Now, Pap."


I DID NOT attend the execution, obviously. Even I knew it was impossible. The man did die, though. His name was in the paper, not his picture, which meant he was a black man. I cried my guts out when I heard about it. Right in front of my father I turned on the television and watched Pearl Bailey sing "Won't You Come Home, Bill Bailey" and said, "She's pretty." My father left the room in disgust and got so drunk he had to be taken to the hospital to have his stomach pumped. I had always known he drank because of me, and for the first time I didn't care. I wished he would die and then I cried my guts out about that too. My mother said, "If anybody asks you, just say he got food poisoning." My grandfather said, "If he was blind, he would have something to get drunk about." I said, "If it was food poisoning going to kill him, he'd been dead long time ago." My mother looked at me like this. I looked right back and double-dog-dared her to say a word and she didn't.

You might as well know the end of this. What is the point of dragging it out? I got up from the dinner table that night and left the house without speaking to anyone. I walked straight to the Baptist church and climbed into the loft and, with a four-foot board, I swatted down a metallic-colored pigeon from the rafters and stomped it till its hard eyes popped out, and pulled out all its feathers and stuffed them in my mouth and puked and swore I would never say, not even to condemn it as evil, the word nigger for the rest of my life. Today, for the one millionth time, as I tell this story, I am breaking that vow. I have no explanations. To seal the vow I pulled down from a corner of the church loft a wasp nest, papery and alive with terrified little red dive-bombers, and squeezed the fiery nest in my hand until my hand was filled with poison and big as a football and I was stung many times all over my body. I also vowed to catch the train. This has no explanation either. I had been wearing a steel beanie and a steel cuff on my leg all my life. I had been eating my last meal forever, and it was not what I ordered. Goodbye, I'm leaving, I'm gone.

I SLEPT in my bed that night and caught the train the next day and rode it forty hard miles. I was sick with fever from the wasp stings. My damaged hand glowed like a bulb. I could scarcely cling to the ladder of the boxcar. I could still taste pigeon feathers in my mouth and throat.

A thousand times, when the train slowed or stopped, I thought of jumping off. I wanted to die in a ditch. I wanted to disappear. I wanted a different history and geography. In rhythm with the wheels I said *I want I want I want I want* I stayed on the train. I breathed the hot exhaust from the diesel. I clung with my one good hand to the ladder and a part of me dreamed a joyful waking dream of falling beneath the wheels. Once, at a cattle crossing, where the train slowed, two children threw rocks at me, and one of the rocks hit my bad hand. The pain of loss and hopelessness caused by that lucky shot was inseparable from my father's drunkenness and the big Philco and Stan the Man. I yelled at the children, "Niggers!" The train slogged on down the line. I yelled, "You could put somebody's eye out!" I laughed my damn head off when I heard myself say this. I sounded just like my mother. I thought of my blind grandfather and Sammy Davis, Jr. I was a sick and bitter child.

Later that day, delirious with fever and loss, I stepped off the train into a cinder lot in sight of the Mississippi River. I did not even look at the river. I had escaped nothing, proved nothing. I walked far across the train yard until I came to a warehouse with baggage carts parked beside it. Under one of the carts was a black man having an epileptic seizure. It lasted a long time, and all I knew to do was stand and watch. I had never heard the word epilepsy at this time. I was so sick I actually thought for one second that I was at home in my bed having a nightmare about living in the house with my family. When the seizure ended the man slept and snored and finally woke up and sat up for a while with his face in his hands. At last he struggled to his knees and then to his feet, and set out across the lot with a slow and wobbly gait. Behind him I called, "I'm sorry!" I sat down where he had been sitting, under the baggage cart. I thought of the long black train. I thought of bean fields and rice paddies and buckshot and gumbo. I lay down and believed that I would die. I suffered chills and fever, and I slept two hours of black sleep before I woke, feeling better.

And now here is a strange thing. In fact, it's the strangest thing I know of.

When I woke up, no one was nearby. The cinder lot was

deserted. I looked around for the man who had suffered the seizure, but he was gone, of course. I walked out of the railroad yard and down long sad streets of shanties. I lost sight of the big river.

I came to a small café with a sign that said REGAL. It was owned by a skinny white-trash man with a big Adam's apple and a yellow dog.

The man looked at me. I was black with cinders and train filth. The man let me use the telephone.

I said, "Mama?"

My mother said, "Sugar?"

I said, "I'm filthy and I'm hungry and I'm sick and I want to die. I watched a man have a fit."

My mother said, "Sugar-man, your grandfather can *see*! It's a miracle."

I said, "I'm in Greenville. Can you come get me?"

She said, "Of course we can, Sugar-man, but aren't you happy? Your grandfather who was blind is no longer blind and now can see. It's like the Bible."

I said, "Something worked."

My mother said, "I think it's love. Love is always the answer."

The white-trash man with the yellow dog said, "I wouldn't want to rush you, son, but like the poet said, Time is money."

I hung up and said, "My grandfather's sight came back. He was blind until today."

The white-trash man took a big handful of the skin of the dog's back in his hand and gave it a couple of good yanks. The dog looked back over its shoulder at the man, lovingly, and the man yanked the dog's skin again. The man said, "Your grand-daddy ain't the first white man to get cured for spite."

I said, "He'll have to learn how to watch television."

The white-trash man said, "You ort to get somebody to look at that hand." He said, "Don't be touching my dog, I wouldn't want it to catch nothing." This was a joke, so we both laughed. The yellow dog ambled over to me and so I sat in a chair and gathered the dog's skin into my good hand and gave it a few good yanks.

I said, "So you're saying spite works?"

The white-trash man said, "You bet. Spite works when nothing else won't."

The white-trash man gave me two big gulps out of a bottle of sweet wine and so I felt better. I thought of the train. The train ride seemed to have taken place in another life. I thought of the crossing signals. I thought of the arms of the semaphore. I thought of the mileposts. I thought of the click of the rails, the jingle of the wheels. I thought of the many little stations I had passed—Quito, and Colony Town, and Victim, and Cruger. I thought of women in headrags picking wild fruit into clean lard buckets along the tracks. When I thought of these things, with the red wine in my stomach and the yellow dog beneath my hand, I was a happy child and the world was a place of safety and peace.

THERE IS one more thing to tell. Many days later, when my illness was coming to an end, and the bandages were removed from my infected hand, I was lying in bed between clean sheets and with my head on two fluffed-up pillows my mother had put there, my grandfather, who now could see, came into my room and sat in a chair beside my bed. He had never done such a thing before.

Then he moved from the chair and actually sat on the bed itself, right beside me. I have to tell you, I was frightened. He could have said anything in the world to me. He could have killed me this day with his bitterness.

He said, "Sugar, long time ago there was a man name of Harper. This is when I was a boy. Harper had a friend who was a midget. Harper and the midget were violent men, don't ask me why, I can't explain. One time the midget held a dog on a rope and Harper poured gas on it and they set the dog on fire. Dog name of Holyghost, don't ask me why, I can't explain that neither. I started to watch Harper and the midget. I watched them drink coffee in the Delta Cafe. I watched them run trotlines on Roebuck and on Quiver River. I watched them drink whiskey. I watched them cut wood with a chainsaw. One day Harper lost control of the chainsaw and accidentally cut off his own hand. I watched him do that too. The midget drove him in the pickup to Dr. Hightower's office, and Harper lived and so did the midget, of course. But they forgot to take the hand. I got the hand. I brushed the sawdust off. I gave it a firm handshake. I waved bye-bye to Harper with it. I played peep-eye behind it. I sang 'Take My Hand, Precious Lord.' I picked my nose with it. I bit its fingernails. I scratched my ass with it. I said, 'Gimme five.' I said, 'Lend me a hand.' I saluted the flag. I yanked a yellow dog. I shot the bird. I thumbed my nose. I thumbed a ride. I took it to a palm reader. I said, 'Read this, sister.'" My grandfather said, "Do you see what I mean?"

I said, "That's why you are a bad man?"

He said, "Yes."

I said, "And that's why Daddy is an idiot?"

He said, "Yes."

I said, "And what about me?"

He said, "I don't know."

I thought of Holyghost burning alive. I thought of the soft fragrances of swamp water and wood rot. I thought of cypress and mimosa. I'm still thinking of those things today. I'm still asking the same question, though my father and grandfather are a long time dead: What about me?

# The Cellar of Runt Conroy

THE ONLY house in the Mississippi Delta with a full basement was a rambling many-roomed tar-paper shack owned by Roy Dale's daddy, a white-trash gentleman named Runt Conroy. Runt was weasely and drawn and he worked, when he was sober enough, as a backhoe driver, digging sewers and graves and ditches for pipelines. It was his own hands that had dug the basement of the Conroy shanty.

There was a passel of Conroy children, all red-haired and sunken-cheeked. I was never really sure how many. There were the twin girls, Cloyce and Joyce, children who spoke in unison. There was a misfit child named Jeff Davis who believed his pillow was on fire. And, of course, there was the boy near my age, Roy Dale, and a very young child, about four, named Douglas, whose only ambition when he grew up was to become an apple. There were others who were grown and had moved away.

Mrs. Conroy, the mother, was an angry woman. She seemed especially angry at Douglas, the child of low ambition. She berated him for it. She encouraged him to want to be something finer than an apple. She threatened to beat him if he did not change his mind. "You will always be white trash," she said to this four-year-old child. "You will never amount to anything. Do you want to be a doctor?" "Apple," Douglas replied. "Do you want to be a policeman? A fireman? A cowboy? A secretary?" "Apple," he replied each time. With enough effort she could wear Douglas down. With enough nagging he would change. Once he upgraded his ambition to a level that almost satisfied her. "Do you want to be a bootlegger? A pimp? A computer scientist?" "All right," Douglas said at last. "I don't want to be an apple." Mrs. Conroy was happy, she was a new woman, she was elated. She said, "I knew it! I was right after all, my darling boy, my own true son! You are not like the rest of the Conroys, you are not white trash. You are a wonderful child, the hope of our family." Douglas said, "I want to grow up to be a dog." It didn't matter. Mrs. Conroy was not dejected. Dog was not good, but it was progress. Dog was better than apple. Other days were less joyous. Other days Douglas would slip backwards. Once he wanted to be a cork. That night his mother cried herself to sleep while Runt sat lovingly beside her bed and wrung his hands and said, "He could do worse, darling, he could do a lot worse."

Most of the Conroy children were filthy and ragged and had sores on their legs, and skin like alligator hide. One of them was different, Dora Ethel, a teenaged girl in perfect health who wore immaculate clothes and Woolworth makeup and made good grades in school, the freak of the family. She went out on dates.

My own family was poor, but this did not keep us from

looking down on the Conroys and sneering when they took canned goods from the Episcopal charity box at Christmas.

Mrs. Conroy—Fortunata was her name—was a teacher's aide in an elementary school some ten miles away. She was not an attractive woman. She had a horsey face and buck teeth and a voice like sheet metal. Most of the children she taught were poor blacks, scared little first graders with no telling what kinds of homes in the swamp. She was gentle but not warm to them. In the middle of a reading lesson, when any person on earth might least expect it, let alone a small peasant child faced with reading a language scarcely his own, Fortunata Conroy would suddenly look up at the small quivering sea of little black faces and she would say in her impossible voice, "God has denied me two gifts, beauty and a pleasing voice," and without another word would turn back to the struggle of sounding out the meaningless words of the stories the children were pretending to read. Fortunata was jealous and believed that every other woman in town was sexually attracted to her weasely husband Runt.

I had been inside the Conroy home a few times, but only briefly and never to take a meal or to spend a night. Roy Dale never invited me to sleep over. He had a million excuses—the small space, the lack of hot water and meals, his meddlesome sisters, the single bathroom, even the possibility of rats. Neither Roy Dale nor I ever mentioned the real concern, that Roy Dale was ashamed of his family.

Finally I wore him down. When you can manipulate a person with nothing else, you give him your secrets. I told Roy Dale that my father drank and was often depressed and maybe even suicidal. Roy Dale did not believe me but he had sense enough to know that such an admission, even if it was false, required reciprocation.

"My daddy wants to die," I said.

"Want to sleep over?" he replied.

THE CONROY home was a shack, but it was not small. There was one impossible room after another. The floors were covered with yellow linoleum, some of the rooms were papered with newspaper. There were dangerous-looking space heaters in many rooms. The pictures on the walls were of Blue Boy and of a wolf standing on a snowy hillside looking at a house. They had been cut out of a magazine and stuck in cheap frames. I pretended to love the wolf picture. For effect I said, "Sometimes that's the way I feel." Roy Dale gave me a look, but he didn't accuse me of lying.

The real reason I wanted to visit here was that I was interested in the Conroys' cellar. I had never seen a cellar before. The word itself impressed me. Cellar, root cellar, storm cellar. The cellar was the one detail of the Conroys' lives that almost rescued them, in my mind at least, from the charge of white trash.

Fortunata Conroy, Roy Dale's mother, did not agree. She

hated the cellar. It reminded her of Runt. Runt had dug it. It was a sewer, it was a ditch, it was a grave. It was an underground monument to white-trashery. Nobody should have a cellar. Having a cellar was proof positive to Fortunata Conroy that their genes and chromosomes were tainted. A billion dollars, a college education, and new teeth would not save a family from white-trash chromosomes if they were the only family in the Mississippi Delta with a cellar. Cellars stunk. Cats pissed in cellars. Potatoes rotted in them. Cellars were homes for rats.

Each day when Fortunata came home from work she walked into the house in search of evidence against herself and Runt. Her nose twitched, her entire face vibrated with accusation. And each day when she arrived home she said the same thing: "This place stinks!"

It was partly true. The incredible sea-level cellar could not be expected to hold out moisture. There was mildew built into the architecture. And the Conroys also had an old cat who sometimes peed in the basement, and especially on damp days a smell of urine could be detected in the air. "This place stinks!" Fortunata would say, and the cat and Runt and the whole gaggle and pride of viral and damaged children would leap for cover. At one time the Conroys had a parrot that could speak not a word but could make a sound like a cash register. It lived in the cellar until its feathers changed color and fell out. That, however, is another story.

The effluvium of the cellar was not really related to mildew or the cat; it was an accusation of Runt for his alcoholism, his birthright, his genes, his occupation, his adulteries real or imagined, his very breath. "This place stinks!" The house rang with the bad music of that refrain. "This place stinks!" The smell, real or imagined, was Runt's fault. Runt believed this as thoroughly as Fortunata.

He sniffed the cellar daily for the place where the cat was doing her evil business.

It was a day in April that I came to spend the night with Roy Dale and his family. It was this same day that Runt put forth his best effort to correct the smell in the basement.

He filled a yellow plastic bucket with hot water from the laundry tub and poured in a dollup of Parson's pine-scented ammonia. Roy Dale and I sat on the cellar steps and watched Runt the way normal children watch television. Runt swished the foamy water around with his hand and breathed the chemical fragrance into his nostrils. He began his search for cat piss.

He sniffed the fabric of a discarded chair near the useless hot water heater. He poked through a sad heap of linoleum scraps and cardboard boxes and cheap suitcases and round hat boxes containing veiled remnants of Fortunata's millinery past— and through newspapers and cinder blocks and a cracked mirror and the rags-and-tags of children's clothing, looking for the smell. He found nothing unusual, no cat piss, but he was not discouraged.

He tilted the yellow bucket so that the chemical water flowed over the basement floor. He had a new brush with yellow plastic bristles.

When he was finished his undershirt was sweaty and his knees were wet. He wiped sweat from his forehead with his scrawny scaly forearm. He looked satisfied.

Roy Dale had said nothing at all during the whole time Runt had been working. Suddenly now he said, "It stinks!" He meant the pine-scented ammonia cleanser.

Runt looked up. He forced a pained smile. He said, "It smells kind of refreshing though, don't it? Kind of pine forest clean?"

Roy Dale said, "It stinks! Ugh! It stinks!" Then he jumped up and ran up the stairs, holding his nose in an extravagant way. I leaped up and followed him. I held my nose also and said, "Ugh! Gag! It stinks!" I understood that there is something about seeing a wounded man that makes you want to hurt him.

For that reason it is hard for me to think of Fortunata Conroy, for all her meanness, as an evil woman. In fact, I believe she loved Runt and all her strange children. I think her intentions were always better than her actions.

Now when I look back on this day I think of Fortunata getting off work that afternoon at the elementary school in Leflore. I imagine that her classroom is neat and orderly, unlike her out-of-control tar-paper house and life. I imagine that the chalkboards are washed and the erasers are clean. I imagine that she puts an extra thumbtack in a colorful poster on the bulletin board. There are health charts and dental-hygiene reminders and smiling Dr. Seuss monsters with good advice. *Stop Look Listen    Be A Friend    Don't Talk To Strangers* I imagine Fortunata grading the last of the first-grade writing papers. She brings the hump of an *f* up to the top of a line; she extends the tail of a *g* to the line below. She checks the pregnant hamster for babies, she grieves the dying Gila monster in the terrarium.

I imagine Fortunata driving home through the incredible flatscape of the Delta. She drives an ancient explosive Pinto beneath wide blue Mississippi skies. She smells the fragrance of cotton flowers on the breeze, she breathes the sweet swamp water of the rice paddies, she passes bean fields shrouded in dragonflies, a pasture with a white mule, the town dump where the rats are as big as collies, past a herd of deer in cornstalks, a dead armadillo on the berm, a flash and sudden clattering of swamp-elves through the brush and across a highwater bridge. The explosive Pinto is a spiritual thing. She is in love with her husband. Her children are normal children. She passes the local stick-fighting team, the high school arrow-catching team on a farther field. She watches old Mr. O'Kelly carve soap on his front porch, and she sees the ventriloquist's dummy named Joseph of Arimethea that poor Mr. O'Kelly believes is his grandson. Mavis Mitchum, a neighbor woman, sucks her skirt. Joby Conroy, Roy Dale's cousin, chases cars.

Mr. Love's goat walks across the mantelpiece in praise. Parrots ring out a wealth of good news. Fortunata is beautiful, her voice is a melody, and she is coming home to the man she loves.

And then she pulls into her driveway and remembers that Runt is probably drunk, has probably already betrayed her today with another woman, or several, that Jeff Davis is trying to extinguish his pillow, and Douglas is a child of low ambition. Before she has set the emergency brake of the car, she can already smell the cellar. The cellar stinks.

These are her first words as she enters the house. "This place stinks!" she says, as if the cotton flowers and the tidy schoolroom had never existed. "This place stinks to high heaven!" she says. Her voice is the wheels of a braking freight train, metal on metal, alarm and dangerous discord. God has denied Fortunata two gifts and Fortunata is here to prove it.

Runt was already defeated. Even Fortunata's voice and angry manner could not have made this more clear. Today of all days it was impossible to deny that the house stunk. It stunk worse than cat piss. It stunk worse than architectural mildew. It stunk as if an ammonia bomb had been exploded in a pine tree.

"This place stinks!" Fortunata said once again for emphasis.

She dropped her plastic briefcase onto a chair where the guiltless cat lay sleeping. The cat shot off the chair and down the cellar stairs, for what reason only God knows. Fortunata glared at Runt. Runt was responsible for the cat. It was a white-trash cat. This is what Fortunata's look told me.

Runt was glum. He said, "I scrubbed the basement floor." It was an apology and an admission of guilt.

Fortunata said, "My God, what did you *use!*"

Runt was hidden inside his own head. His eyes peered out of a skull. He looked like a rat in a soup can.

I was frightened of what might happen next. I said to Roy Dale, "Want to go outside?"

I could hear Jeff Davis far away in his room. "Fire!" he called out. "Man the hoses!" Jeff Davis was a madman, but he was also a practical joker. It was never clear to me when he was in psychosis and when he was a comedian. Runt knew, though. Runt, even in terror of Fortunata's wrath, could laugh a sweet and fatherly laugh at this dark joke of a little boy. Runt said, with sincerity, "We are a lucky family."

Fortunata was having none of it. She said again, "What did you *use?*" Speaking of the ammonia bomb.

Jeff Davis called out, "Bucket brigade!"

Fortunata said, "What did you use to make this house stink?"

Runt said, "A good deal of time and energy."

I could look into Fortunata Conroy's eyes and know that she hated herself for this scene. I knew that she heard the impossibly harsh, hard metallic grating of her voice. I knew that she believed it was scenes such as this that gave her this voice, not genetics or even bad luck but only bitterness and a heart too long hardened by fear and rage and outrage. She knew how thoroughly out of line with her vision of marriage and joy and hope this scene fell and also that she was responsible for it. And yet she could not stop. In her mind swamp-elves bolted from cover and crossed a glen and into the trees and cane.

"Gallop the horses! Hook and ladders!" called Jeff Davis from his room.

Fortunata did not hold back on account of me. This open fighting told me that she was white trash to the core. A family of higher quality would have died before allowing me, an outsider, to witness their anger and pain. She said to Runt, "You worthless failure. You stinking drunk. You impotent pig."

I heard a voice say, "I like the way it smells."

It was Roy Dale. We were standing together in the room, practically clinging to each other. There were framed pictures of the entire white-trash family on the mantel above the living room space heater. Generations of rednecks in black and white and sepia and even in color. Aunts and uncles and cousins, nephews and nieces, foundlings and mulattoes, Ku Kluxers and gentle parsons. There were rednecks behind the traces of a mule, rednecks beneath false bowers at the senior prom, rednecks at weddings, rednecks in academic regalia at Ole Miss, rednecks in flannel shirts and fake pearls and with stethoscopes around their necks. There was enough money in professional photography of rednecks to fill in the miserable cellar with dirt and bury Runt and the cat in the bargain.

When Roy Dale said, "I like the way it smells," all the rest of the people in the room, including myself, looked at him as if he were a man from Mars.

Nothing could stop Fortunata Conroy, or so I believed. She said, "I'll tell you why this house stinks."

Runt said, "Shut your ugly mouth."

Fortunata was momentarily stopped. She said, "What did . . ."

Runt said, "Your voice is like eating ground glass."

Fortunata said, "Don't you dare . . ."

Runt said, "Your breath is like Gary, Indiana."

Fortunata said, "If you ever . . ."

Runt said, "Your tongue is a snake that swallowed a frog."

Then Roy Dale's voice again: he said, "It smells like pine trees to me."

Runt said, "Your gums are raw liver."

Roy Dale said, "I sincerely like the smell of pine trees."

Jeff Davis was silent.

Fortunata said, "You low-life drunk."

Runt said, "You stooge."

Fortunata said, "You sexless lump, you eunuch."

Runt said, "You bitch."

Fortunata said, "Hit me! That's what you want to do! Hit me! It would be a relief!"

Runt said, "You sick slut."

Fortunata was screaming now. She said, "Get out! Go away! I don't want you near these children! Go to a mental hospital!"

Runt said, "Then I would be near your entire family."

Jeff Davis remained quiet. Even Jeff Davis could not be in a good mood all the time.


RUNT WENT away from the house then. We heard the front screen door slap shut and then the Pinto started up. There was no explosion. Roy Dale led me out of the living room and down a dark hall to the room where he usually slept. Douglas, the child who wanted to be an apple, was sitting on an army cot, crying.

Roy Dale said, "What's your problem?"

Douglas said, "I don't know."

Roy Dale said, "Me and Sugar want to be alone."

Douglas said, "Ask me what I want to be when I grow up."

Roy Dale said, "I'll ask you tomorrow."

Douglas said, "Ask me now."

Roy Dale said, "What do you want to be when you grow up?"

Douglas stopped crying. He was about four and had a round moonlike face, streaked with dirt. He said, "Apple."

This was a joke the two of them seemed to share.

Roy Dale smiled and said, "Okay now, take off."

Douglas said, "Ask me the next part."

Roy Dale sighed. He said, "Do you want to be a cowboy?"

Douglas said, "No. Apple."

Roy Dale said, "A fireman?"

Douglas was giggling now. He said, "Apple."

Roy Dale said, "Astronaut?"

Douglas said, "Apple. Now say the best part."

Roy Dale said, "You've got no ambition."

Douglas said, "Say the next part. Say it right." Douglas was laughing now, really hard. He lay down on the cot and kicked his feet while he laughed.

Roy Dale said, "You'll always be white trash."

Even Roy Dale was laughing now. Both of them were cracking up. Douglas laughed so hard he got the hiccups and Roy Dale had to say, "Boo!"

Douglas said, "Okay, okay, I don't want to be an apple any more." Both of them were tickled but they were holding back.

This was their favorite part. Roy Dale perfectly imitated his mother's metallic voice: "My darling ambitious child!" he mugged. "My sweetest, most normal, most non–white-trash little angel!" he said, in his mother's voice. "What *do* you want to be when you grow up?"

Now both of them were rolling on the army cot. They were pounding each other on the back. They fell on the floor. They

were hysterical. Douglas tried several times and was too tickled to speak. At last he blurted it out: "I want to be a dog!"
They hooted, they screamed, they guffawed, they chortled and
lost their breath.

And then Douglas dried his eyes and got up off the floor. He
was finished with the laughter. Roy Dale watched him, looking for something, I'm not sure what.

Douglas said, "That was a bad one." He meant the fight
between Runt and Fortunata.

Roy Dale said, "Your tongue is the snake that swallowed
a frog."

Douglas did not laugh. He said, "Yeah. Right." And then
went on to bed in another room.

IT WAS a good night for me to spend the night away from
home. A steady rain had begun to fall and the clouds were dark
and as low as the cottonwood trees in the bare grassless yard.
Roy Dale and I sat alone in his room and played cards with a
greasy deck of Bicycles and listened to the rain in the trees and
on the roof and heard it puddle up in the yard. Life in the
Conroy family went on and rarely touched the two of us. Sup-
per was never mentioned, and my stomach gnawed on its own
emptiness. It felt good to be hungry and to expect no food to
relieve the hunger. It was easy to pay the small price of a
night's hunger for the sweet isolation that Roy Dale and I were

allowed to share. It frightened me to enjoy these moments with a white-trash child who, until now, I had believed was put upon earth only for my manipulation.

A few times family members stopped by our door and looked in. The twins who spoke in unison stopped for a moment and said nothing. Cloyce and Joyce.

At last Roy Dale said, "You can't come in here."

In unison they said, "We know that." They shared their mother's nasality, but in them it was sweet beyond belief.

Roy Dale said, "Sugar is my friend, not yours."

In one voice they said, "We know that."

Roy Dale said, "You're not really talking at the same time. Cloyce is talking first and Joyce is talking right behind."

In perfect duet they said, "You think you are so smart, Mr. Smartypants." Then they went away.

Roy Dale said, "Just be lucky you don't have sisters."

Later Dora Ethel, the freak sister who wore makeup and got good grades, stopped at Roy Dale's door. She said, "Hey, Sugar." Talking to me.

Dora Ethel was very pretty and I was surprised to find myself speechless and in love. I said, "Huh, huh, huh." She said, "You're cute." The rain was drumming on the house. It was a tropical rain, a jungle rain. There was a prophet's voice in the rain. It said: *You will grow up to marry a white-trash girl* Water stains were broadening across the ceiling.

Dora Ethel really wanted to speak to Roy Dale, though.

She said, "I'm going out."

Roy Dale said, "So?"

Dora Ethel said, "So, look, I'm taking Daddy's pistol, okay? Don't tell, all right, but that's where it is."

Roy Dale said, "Got a date?"

Dora Ethel took the pistol out of her skirt pocket and twirled it on her finger in a funny little sexy way. She said, "Ask me no questions, I'll tell you no lies." Dora Ethel was by far the cutest white-trash person I had ever seen.

When she was gone I said, "She takes a pistol on a date?"

Roy Dale said, "She goes with Grease Hodges. They shoot rats at the dump."

I said, "That's what she does on a date?"

Roy Dale said, "When it rains like this, yeah."

I said, "Shoots rats on a date? That's what she does?"

Roy Dale was not defensive. He said, "Her and Grease. It's something they like to do together."

I said, "Grease Hodges?"

Roy Dale let it drop. My heart ached with jealousy. I would never be old enough to leave the house beneath an apple-green night sky in a tropical storm, never old enough to love a girl who twirled a pistol on her finger, or to shoot rats at the dump for love. My genes had become infected with Conroy genes. I was terrified of the transformation, and I gloried in it.

No one came in later to tell us good night. One by one the children put themselves to bed. Lights went out. Runt's Pinto never returned, though Runt did, on foot. Maybe that was the night the Pinto exploded. Or maybe it only stalled out in the deep rain water in the street. In any case, Runt came home, and there was no more fighting.

Roy Dale took off his clothes and lay on the bed naked, so I got naked too, and together we lay and listened to the drumming insistent rain. The yard outside our window was a lake. Douglas, who usually slept on the army cot, slept somewhere else tonight. We turned off the electric bulb hanging from a cord in the middle of the room and lay in the loud sounds of constant tons of falling water. Even Dora Ethel finally came in, dripping wet, and skulked through the house trying to replace Runt's pistol without being seen. The room was not entirely dark. There were streetlights far away, and the light from Red's All Night Bar at the end of the street. I could see Roy Dale place his hand between his legs, and so in a short time I placed my hand between my legs too, and we lay and breathed and did not speak.

It was very late now. So much time passed that I thought Roy Dale might be asleep. He said, "Runt has slept with two-hundred and seventy different women."

I said, "Slept with them?"

He said, "I found a list of their names."

I was beginning to catch on to what "slept with them" meant.

I thought about this for a while. I said, "Can I see it?—
the list?"

He said, "It's in the back of Runt's closet in a box."

I said, "My daddy hides a rock-and-roll suit in the back of
his closet. It's black and it's got Rock-n-Roll Music spelled out
on the back in little glittery things, sequins."

Roy Dale said, "Do you want a rubber? I stole some from
Runt's drawer." He reached under his mattress and took out a
few foil-wrapped packets.

I said, "Naw, thanks. Daddy's got plenty. I blow them up.
Put water in them. You know."

Roy Dale said, "You ought to try jacking off in one sometime. It adds a little something."

I said, "Hm."

We were silent again. The sound of the rain was without
thunder. It was as constant as the feeling of loss that suddenly I
felt inside me, that now I knew had been with me all along, a
familiar part of me since the beginning of memory.

Roy Dale said, "Jeff Davis can pull a condom down over
his head."

I turned and looked at Roy Dale in the weird green light of
the storm sky. I said, "Get real."

He said, "No, really. All the way down over his face. Ears
and everything."

I turned and looked up at the dripping ceiling. I said,
"Caramba."

Roy Dale said, "He pretends he's robbing a 7-Eleven. Mama won't let him use one of her stockings."

I said, "That's really crazy, Roy Dale."

He said, "Right, I know. You can smother with a condom pulled over your head."

I said, "Caramba," again.

He said, "I know."

I said, "You would look pretty funny, you know, sticking up a store with a rubber over your head."

Roy Dale said, "It would be on the ten o'clock news. 'Two Caucasian males wearing condoms over their heads . . .'" We laughed pretty hard at this. We tried not to wake anybody up, but we were pretty tickled, I can tell you.

I said, "You wouldn't be able to talk. You couldn't say 'Stick 'em up.'"

Roy Dale said, "You'd have to go, 'Ump ump ump.'"

We laughed our damn heads off. We said, "Shh, shh!" And then we laughed some more.

THERE IS not much more to tell. The storm outside was without wind and without lightning or thunder. The rain fell straight down and its falling did not diminish. The sound was constant, a pounding like heavy hammers that we could forget to hear. For a long time Roy Dale and I said nothing. He lay on his back, and I lay on my back. He did not touch himself and did not move. His breathing was soft and regular and I thought again he might be asleep. In the stillness a thought came to me like a friendly voice. The voice said: *We are all alone in this world*

Just then Roy Dale said, "Your daddy has got a rock-and-roll suit?"

I turned my head in his direction and could see his body outlined in the green light of the storm-sky outside the window. I said, "In the back of his closet."

Roy Dale said, "So, like, what does he do?—like, puts it on and dances around, or what?"

I said, "I don't know. I don't think so. I think he just, you know, *has* it."

Roy Dale said, "Will you let me see it?"

I thought about this. No one had ever seen the rock-and-roll suit but me. I sneaked looks at it when no one else was in the house. Still I said, "I guess so."

Roy Dale said, "Great."

I said, "We wouldn't be, you know, like making fun of him or anything."

Roy Dale said, "No way. Uh-uh."

I said, "Well, okay, yeah, sure. I'll show it to you sometime."

Roy Dale said, "Tonight?"

I said, "Tonight?"

Roy Dale settled back on his pillow. He said, "You're right, it's a bad idea."

I said, "No, it's all right. We could do it tonight."

We did not go out that night, of course. We only lay in the dark and in the sound of the rain.

In a while Roy Dale said, "Come on," and the two of us stepped out of bed and moved quietly through the house and opened the cellar door. We were careful to wake no one. Jeff Davis might have called for the pumper trucks, the REO Speedwagon. Douglas might have wanted to be an apple. Cloyce and Joyce might have god-knows-what, in unison. Dora Ethel might have broken my heart. Roy Dale had a flashlight, which he shined into the darkness. At first I could see nothing, only the sturdy solid beam of light like a long pole. I followed behind Roy Dale, through the cellar door, down the steps, only two or three steps down before he stopped. He sat and I sat beside him.

Roy Dale shined the light out into the basement and I understood for the first time what I was looking at, not mere blackness but deep water. The basement was four or five feet deep in rainwater. Roy Dale swept the light back and forth across it. I might as well have been Hernando DeSoto discovering the Father of Waters, the mighty Mississippi, for all my amazement at the sight. It was an interior sea, an indoor elementary mystery as dangerous and filled with evil meaning as any cavern, any water-filled cavity of the underworld.

Then on the face of the deep I thought I could see something else, some moving thing, or things. I imagined eyeless fish, I imagined mermaids, I heard their song. Roy Dale caught them in the beam of his flashlight. Earnest little faces and diamond-bright eyes, moving through the water, swimming for dear life, no doubt, but as if for pleasure. It was rats. A dozen or more of them. Large doglike barn rats, swimming quietly and without desperation along the black surface of this cellar sea.

Roy Dale said, "If Runt was awake he might let us shoot them with his pistol."

We took turns holding the flashlight on their sweet earnest evil little comical faces. I thought of the collie-size rats at the town dump. They were burrowed deep in the garbage. They were waiting for the rain to end. I thought of that time a few hours from now, when this jungle storm would be finished. I thought of the Delta moon shining in the after-storm sky, with its ragged slow-moving clouds. I imagined the collie rats creeping from their hiding places in the rank waste-pits of human misery and into the soft air. I saw them sit along riverbanks and scratch behind an ear or shake rainwater from their fur. I saw the collie-rats look up at the miraculous moon and howl and bay at its light. They barked and sang like mythical beasts and I heard the little town of Arrow Catcher, Mississippi, fill up with their strange rodent harmony. I thought of the swamp-elves, happy in their marshy cozy dens. The deer bedded down in cane, the muskrats and the beavers and the ropey-whiskered catfish in the mud. One of us held the flashlight on the little swimmers while the other pointed a finger like a pistol and made pistol sounds—balooey, or ptoosh, or blammo!—and we passed the night in the belief that feeling love for each other and for this single incredible moment in time was all in the world that was important, and that it needed no acknowledgement, not even with a single word.

Later, when we had finished the game and only sat and shined the light onto the water, the old cat crept down the stairs and passed the two of us on the steps, first holding her tail up as she rubbed past, and then going all the way down to the last step visible above the surface of the waves. Roy Dale held the light on her, and we watched her test the water only once, briefly, one second, with one paw, before entering it in a kind of slow, mad cat-dive outwards, sploosh. The cat swam out into the cellar sea, holding her head high above the water and then relaxing some and swimming with confidence and ease. She was trying to corner one of the rats in the flood. Roy Dale and I cheered the cat. We shouted whispered directions—"This way!" and "Behind you!"—and we tried to direct the cat to individual rats with the beam of the flashlight. It was no use. The cat was a good swimmer but no match for the experienced rats. This was their home, and there were frequent heavy rains in the Delta. Finally she gave up and left

the water, back up the steps the way she had come, defeated
and cranky and soaking wet, not even shaking herself to dry
her fur. An apathetic, lazy, white-trash cat.

Roy Dale and I were finished. We were tired and sleepy. We
turned off the flashlight and went back up the stairs. Roy Dale
eased shut the cellar door, so that no one heard. We went to
bed then and snuggled close to each other. I felt his rough
white-trash alligatory skin against my own softer skin and was
comfortable and drowsy and I listened to the rain and I knew
that it was falling more softly now, coming to an end, and that
tomorrow everything that had been thrown underneath my
own home a few blocks away—the empty whiskey bottles, the
soup cans and empty paint buckets, a dead battery, a hairless
doll, a slick tire, scraps of paper, indescribable garbage, the ice
pick my father once stabbed himself in the chest with while I
watched him, the towels he bled into as his face turned white
while my mother closed the window shades so that no one else
would see—all this would have been washed out from under
our house by the jungle rain. It would lie in the yard and on
the sidewalk and in the street for anyone to see. And then my
mother would gather it all up again and toss it beneath the
house again, and again we would forget.

I moved my body close to Roy Dale. I reached in the
darkness, afraid even to open my eyes, afraid he would disappear, and I held him to me. I embraced him. I encircled him.

We were like spoons together. We were like swamp-elves. And in this way we went to sleep, bare-assed children, the two of us, and in my memory not blameworthy for any sin and not even victims of the sins of our sad fathers, but, only that moment, in love with what is and what has always been or what might forever be.

# Porpoises and Romance

AFTER THE hurricane, beach houses along the Gulf coast rented for a song, and so that was when my daddy got the idea of taking my mama on a second honeymoon. My mama said she never had a honeymoon in the first place, what did she want with a second one.

Daddy said they would take long walks and watch the sun rise and eat crabs and rent bicycles and browse in shops. He said they would put the zip back in their marriage.

Mama said, "Crabs! No way, José."

Daddy said it would be like having their own private beach.

Mama said, "I don't know why you want to be riding on a bicycle."

He said, "Come on, baby. Let's fall in love all over again."

Mama said, "Well, all right. Can Sugar go along?"

Daddy said, "On our second honeymoon?"

I said, "I ain't studying no second honeymoon."

Mama said, "I'm not going on no second honeymoon less Sugar comes along."

Daddy said, "It don't seem right, falling in love all over again right in front of your own boy."

Daddy was right about one thing anyway. The beach was deserted. It was worse than deserted. The hurricane had blown most of the sand five miles inland, not to mention the hotels. The beaches were mud, the hotels were hideouts for murderers and swamp-midgets. Daddy said, "Well, wouldn't you think they'd have got this place cleaned up a little by now?"

We were standing on the beach, which was filled with dead fish and other animal carcasses, including a whale full of buzzards.

I said, "I'm scared, I want to go home."

Daddy said, "That whale smells like Korea."

Mama said, "Hush up, both of you. Are both of you boys trying to spoil my one and only second honeymoon?"

Daddy looked at me like: duh.

The little coastal village where Mama and Daddy rented the house was a ghost town. Everything was full of sand from the hurricane, even the trees, the ones that were left standing. And you couldn't go barefoot on account of broken glass, you might step on a piece and cut the living daylights out of yourself. It's hard to clean up after a hurricane. Buzzards flew up out of the whale like bats out of a cave.

THE SHOPS were all closed, of course, and so were most of the restaurants. One restaurant still had a palm tree, roots and all, sticking through the busted-out front window. There was a coffee shop where we tried to have breakfast one morning, but the woman behind the counter slammed cups and saucers around like she was mad at us. Daddy whispered to Mama, "I hope she ain't expecting the full ten percent tip."

Even the parking meters had been stripped from their posts and stored away somewhere. Bicycle rental was out of the question, of course. And at night the house we were staying in, which was olive green with muscular mildew and alive with one million crickets in the kitchen cabinets and in the furniture and bathroom and light fixtures, foreign crickets blown in from Tahiti or Cuba on the hurricane, and fungi possibly from other planets, had buzzards roosting on the chimney like a gang of sea gulls gone bad, and it was the only place along the beach with any lights on. We were a lonely lighthouse, we were a ship lost at sea, we were an outpost in Indian Territory. We were one of the few places with a roof.

Mama said, "It's so quiet."

Daddy said, "Yeah." His voice was soft and a little frightened sounding. He said, "It's definitely a quiet little place."

Mock it down: My parents were not falling in love all over again.

It's not that they weren't trying to fall in love. They were trying until they turned blue in the face. It was embarrassing to watch them, Daddy was right about that too.

They said soft things (I just stayed out of their way, I just watched, I just slunk around and spied on them), they brought iced tea to bed with flowers on a tray, they ate dinner by candlelight on the front porch. Picture my daddy, with thirty-five years of housepaint under his fingernails and housepaint on the freckled, veined lids of his eyes, varnish permanent in the pigmentation of his skin, his hair, the color of his eyes, my daddy, with webbed toes on his feet and not one white tooth in his mouth, lighting candles for dinner for the first time in his entire life! It would break your heart to watch him, he was trying so hard to be in love, so desperate now that he knew he was not.

Daddy said, "Listen to the deep voice of the sea tonight." He actually said this, this man who scarcely said hello on all the other days of the year, and the sound of his own voice speaking language near to poetry, near to passion, scared my daddy so bad that he actually leaped straight up off the floor in fear and ran out of the room and flung himself on the bed and cried for a full minute at the shock of it.

Whenever I long for the return of my own innocence, I imagine becoming the person that my strange daddy was in that sixty seconds of his life, and then I have to admit that I was never so innocent, even as a child, no one on this earth ever was so innocent except him. My parents walked on the beach in the moonlight, stepping over strange things they could not see, they agreed on many things, including autumn as their favorite season of the year, and the smell of salt in the sea air. My mother was even beginning to be convinced that this might work, this second honeymoon in search of love.

But then love is cruel, I mean why lie about it.

The second honeymoon was not romantic. It was not working. It had nothing to do with the dead whale, or the other bodies that were beginning to wash up.

So they tried harder.

They played a couple of fantasy games. Daddy had read about sexual fantasies in a magazine called *Connections*. *Connections* was a magazine for people who wanted to put the zip back in their marriage. I had read the fantasies too. I found the magazine in Daddy's room before we ever left home, in the drawer of his bedside table, while I was stealing rubbers to lend to a child who could stretch a condom over his head. I read them while sitting with my pants down around my ankles on the hardwood floor of my room, beating away. It's one of my special childhood memories, sitting bare-assed on wood and holding my life in my hands.

I didn't see my parents play these games, of course, but I know it happened. Daddy tied Mama to the bed posts with four silk ties he had brought along, just for the purpose. Yikes. I found the ties still dangling there like dogs with their tongues hanging out, one morning. One of them had a hand-painted horse's head on it.

Well, I mean, you know. Suicide was one of the thoughts I had.

Mama said all the right things, I suppose, all the words that *Connections* magazine recommended. "Fuck me, master, I'm your slave," and like that. It's embarrassing to think of your mama saying she's a sex slave, you know, but it's not the end of the world. That's the way I thought of it at the time.

*Connections* had some other good ideas, too. *Connections* said that the concerned couple could pretend to be a young boy and his stern high school science teacher. They could use an electric vibrator as a part of the boy's high school science project.

Maybe they did this, maybe not. I looked for something that might be a vibrator, but I'm not sure. I found a device in the back of one of my daddy's dresser drawers, along with a bottle of Four Roses whiskey and a bag of peppermint candy. It might have been a vibrator, or it might have been a curling iron. Who knows? Some things about your parents you can never be sure of.

The thing is, sex was not the only area that *Connections* magazine had suggestions for. It had suggestions in areas far more fantastic than mere sexual playfulness, though that must have been foreign enough to my father.

*Connections* magazine had recommendations for metaphor and romance. It said, "Find a metaphor for romance, and pursue it with all your heart. If your first choice of metaphor fails, keep trying others until you hit upon just the right one for you and your partner."

I actually saw my father sitting on the side of his bed in his room at home reading this particular article. He had no shoes on, he was just home from a long day on an extension ladder, and so he worked his webbed toes against the floor as he read. I stood in the doorway and watched.

He finished the article and shook his head and sighed. He read the article a second time.

At last he looked up from the magazine and saw me. I had already read the article and understood it as little as my daddy did.

I heard a voice say, "What's a queer?"

It was my own voice, of course. What did I mean by asking such a question? It was a question I had often wanted the answer to, but why now, suddenly?

My daddy looked at me with a blank face.

Neither of us said anything for a long time.

Finally he said, "What? What did you say, Sugar?"

I said, "What's a queer?"

Daddy looked back down at *Connections* magazine and read again a part of the article he had just read. He looked back up at me.

I said, "Roy Dale Conroy is such a queer." Roy Dale, the white-trash child, my best friend, the one whose youngest brother could stretch condoms over his head.

Daddy said, "So you are asking me what's a queer, is that it, is that what you are asking?"

I said, "Right."

He sighed and looked down at the article and then back up at me. He said, "Don't say queer, Sugar. Queer is dirty. Roy Dale's not a queer just because his brother can do that trick with the condoms. And a very dangerous trick at that, I might add."

He looked back down at *Connections* magazine and read some more, the same paragraph, over and over.

I said, "Queer is dirty?"

Daddy didn't answer.

I said, "I thought queer meant odd. I thought queer meant Roy Dale is a jerk."

He looked up. He said, "What do you suppose this word means?" He held out the magazine to me and pointed to the page. I walked over to the bed and looked. He was pointing to the word *metaphor*. He said, "It must mean like a sign, a signal of some kind."

I said, "Like from outer space?"

He said, "Yes."

I said, "Like from God?"

He said, "I don't know."

We looked at the word *metaphor* for a long time. Neither of us dared to try to pronounce it. It lay there on the white page being itself, like a signal from outer space.

Daddy tested the word now, mostly to himself. "A mumpty-mump for romance," he mumbled over the word. "A sign from God of romance." He looked up at me, relieved. "Yeah, that's what it means! A sign from God. Right!"

He was very happy. His face was bright. He squinched his webbed toes joyfully on the wood floor.

I didn't know what to say. I said, "What's a queer?"

He said, "Do you know anything about cocksuckers?"

I said, "Some."

He said, "It's the same deal."

I said, "Thanks."

He said, "No problem, don't sweat it, glad to be of help."

SUNRISES. That was the metaphor my daddy chose. Sunrises and romance, he said—that was it, that was just the ticket, sunrises. Now he had looked up the word *metaphor* in the dictionary and was pronouncing it all over the place. Metaphor this, metaphor that, even metaphorical a couple of times. "Sunrises all right with you, honey?" he said to my mother many times. "For a metaphor, I mean? I hope the sunrise metaphor for romance is all right with you. As a metaphor, it's the first metaphor that popped into my head. I mean, what could be more metaphorical than a sunrise, honey, I mean tell the truth? Sunrises are meta-fucking-phorical!"

Mama said, "Don't get carried away, Gilbert."

He said, "Scuse my French!"

Possibly this was one of the happiest days of my daddy's life.

Well, the thing is, sunrises didn't work. My daddy still wasn't falling in love all over again with my mother. And besides, he was always too sleepy and cranky at that time of the morning for anything to have worked.

And then maybe this is where things started to change. My

daddy got it into his head that if he could spot a porpoise, then the love that he and Mama had once shared and now had lost would have swum back to them, alive and renewed in its gentleness.

To be fair to my daddy, the porpoise notion was not as arbitrary as it might sound. Once, a long time ago, before I was ever born, Daddy and some woman—maybe Mama, maybe not, depending on how drunk Daddy was when he told the story—took the ferry to Ship Island one night and stood on the deck with the Gulf breeze in their faces and watched a pair of dolphins follow the ship.

Sometimes when he was very drunk, he would tell me about the lights along that channel, the kerosene smell of the ship's engine, the salt sea air and the porpoises playful in the wake.

So my daddy started to look for porpoises in the dangerous, hurricane-ruined Gulf of Mexico, with blown-out hotels and littered mud beaches and roving gangs of violent teenagers in the abandoned shopping centers and ospreys and oyster-beds and Cajun knife-throwers and swamp-elves in the dark salt-water marshes at his back. He dedicated himself to seeing a porpoise, a metaphor for romance.

I said, "I want to go home. I cut my foot on a piece of glass. They's dead things on the beach. They's a dead man on the beach, washed up there. I don't want to be on a second honeymoon."

He said, "This is the world we live in, Sugar-man. This is the only second honeymoon we'll ever have as a family."

So every morning now Daddy was standing beside the blue Gulf of Mexico in the ruins of southern Mississippi, scanning the horizon and all the breaking waves for some sign of a porpoise.

Always I was awake first, and always I was either with my daddy or behind him, nearby, watching in fear of what all, or any, of this meant.

At times there were other people on the beach. Once there was an old guy surf fishing, and daddy talked to him about porpoises for a while. The old guy baited his dangerous-looking hooks with something slimy from a plastic bucket.

Daddy said, "Do you ever see porpoises out here?"

The old guy said, "I'm thinking about writing a book."

Daddy said, "I read mostly magazines. I'm reading one right now about how to put the zip back in your marriage."

The old guy's pants legs were rolled up and he was barefoot, despite the danger. The tip of his rod bent slightly toward the pull of the waves.

The old guy said, "I've already got a title for it. For this book I'm thinking about writing."

Daddy said, "This magazine, it's called *Connections*. It tells you all about metaphors."

The old guy said, "I'm going to call it *Fun Sex Facts about Animals*."

Daddy said, "Porpoises is my metaphor right now. I'm pursuing porpoises with all my heart, like the magazine says."

The old guy said, "You're actually talking about dolphins. Dolphins are what you see around here. They're bigger than porpoises. The dorsal fin is a little different. And of course they have the beak."

Daddy said, "I haven't had a drink of whiskey since me and my wife and boy left the Delta. No d.t.'s, no hallucinations, nothing."

The old guy said, "The calf is born tail first. That's the fun sex fact about dolphins. That's what I would say about dolphins if I was to write this book I'm telling you about."

Daddy said, "Well, good luck," and started to walk up the filthy beach.

The old guy called after Daddy. He said, "Whale penises are twenty feet long." This is what the old guy shouted to my daddy in the ruins. He shouted, "And bent in the middle."

Daddy waved back in his direction and shrugged as if he could not hear. I was running along trying to catch up now, but I had to be careful of glass in the muddy sand.

The old guy was not finished calling out. He hollered, "Whale vaginas are on the side. That's why the penises are bent, so they can reach around." Ospreys carried silvery fish to their nests in the cypress trees, bodies washed ashore, teenagers drank warm wine in the shopping centers, and God knows what dangerous creatures with scales lay beneath the Gulf waters.

THE NEXT day the ocean seemed paved with silver cobble-stones. If love cannot be summoned by magic or a power of personal will, then at least love's metaphors can be. My mama and my daddy and I were there, wearing our leather shoes and swimsuits on the terrible beach. The pavement of silver in the Gulf was an enormous school of bluefish. There must have been a million of them, literally a million fish, directly on the surface of the water.

And then the porpoises themselves. The sweet hooked fins, the sleek backs and oily humps. My daddy had summoned a school of dolphins. My parents held hands and looked at each other with awe and astonishment.

The dolphins blew like whales. They rolled like wheels. Daddy counted them, but there were too many to count. They bounded, they arched, one of them left the water altogether, and the belly was so white in the sunshine that I wanted to say it was blue.

My daddy looked at my mama with gratitude that amounted to reverence, to religion itself. Porpoises were a perfect meta-phor after all. *Connections* magazine did not lie.

The porpoises were close to the shore. The explosive exhala-tions of their breath! The squeaking and clicking of their voices! Mama and Daddy left me behind and ran together down the corpse-strewn beach, holding hands like movie-star lovers.

It was a porpoise infestation. The incredible school of blue-fish had attracted a hundred or more dolphins, two hundred maybe. There were too many to count. They were crazed. Maybe still psychotic from the effects of the hurricane. I picked my way down the beach, and I could see what my parents saw.

The carnage was spectacular. There were dead fish every-where. Large fish, small fish, parts of fish, fish heads and fish tails and fish guts, fish shit no doubt, washing up onto the beach on every incoming wave.

The porpoises were frightening, there were so many of them, they were so fierce, so large, so mechanical and maniacal in their feeding. They were strong and swift and ruthless and intelligent. The bluefish were hysterical with fear. They were stupid. They were cattle. They were too frightened to dive. They could not get away. They cluttered the surface of the sea.

Now the porpoises could be seen in all their enormity. They were huge. They were eight feet long, nine feet, some of them. They broke the surface, they leaped, they blew spray in spumes from their blowholes. They had a jillion teeth, sharp and dangerous. Their eyes were as hard and as tiny as the eyes of grizzly bears. That is what this was like. Like seeing a hundred, two hundred hungry bears tearing into some frightened frantic grouping of small stupid trapped animals.

Mama said, "What does it mean? What does it mean?"

Daddy said, "Don't look. Let's don't look."

She turned and he held her in his arms.

She said, "I love you."

He said, "I love you."

She said, "Really?"

Now he looked at her.

She had a new red plastic barrette in her hair, and she was sunburned, and she looked like a child.

She said, "Don't tell me you love me if you don't really love me."

I knew I should leave but I did not. I picked up pieces of broken window glass and Coke bottles and sidearmed them at huge dead sea turtles in the sand.

Daddy looked back out at the porpoises.

He said, "Do you love me?"

She said, "Yes. I mean, no. I mean, I don't know. Don't make me answer this." She said, "I can't do this any more. Second honeymoons are just too hard on a girl."

She turned and walked away, up towards the beach house.

Daddy called out to her, angry, hopeless. "Look at this beach!" he said. "Look at it! Porpoises was the best I could do! Porpoises was the best metaphor I could think of!"

My mother kept walking up the filthy sand.

Daddy called, "Jesus Christ, honey! I can't do no better! Maybe if we lived near a better beach!"

THAT'S NOT the end of the story. It seems like it could be, since it's just the kind of thing I'm always hearing myself say these days: If the world were different, I would be different, I would be more in love.

But it's not the end. There is one more thing to tell.

We did not drive back to the Delta that day. We stayed on the coast the whole month. Federal grant money came through while we were still staying at the beach house, and so the bulldozers started up. Cranes with steel balls swung into the walls of buildings and finished the collapse the hurricane had begun. Politicians stumped around making speeches, billboards with clever sayings went up: THE SOUTH SHALL RISE AGAIN. Pumper barges and dredges cleared the Gulf channels and pumped new white sand up onto the beaches. Dead fish and turtles were hauled off in garbage scows, the whale full of buzzards was dragged out to sea by a tugboat. The red lights of ambulances and police cars flashed all night, as the last bodies were carted away to funeral homes. Plate glass in windows was replaced, fallen trees were chainsawed into firewood and stacked in ricks. The ospreys and the swamp creatures lay quiet, quiet in the Mississippi darkness. The knife-throwers went back to New Orleans, the swamp-midgets got work in the construction industry.

My parents and I took long drives in the car and watched the reconstruction. The Gulf coast slowly became beautiful again.

One day as we drove along we realized we had left the state of Mississippi altogether and were actually speeding down a Florida highway, and this made all of us happy, but for some reason it also frightened us, and so Daddy turned the car around and we drove back in the direction of Biloxi and Symbol City and Pass Christian and Gulfport and Pascagoula.

Daddy looked longingly out the car window at house painters on high ladders, brightening the walls and corners of big houses that the hurricane had stripped of paint. He spoke wistfully of possibly moving here, where work was so plentiful, and where the land was so beautiful and the Gulf waters smelled like flowers on the islands beyond the reef.

We kept all the windows of the car rolled down and Mama's hair was beautiful when the wind blew it. Daddy's face got sunburned and his freckles stood out like copper pennies. I found *Connections* magazine in the trash one day, and so I took it out to the dumpster with the shells of shrimp we had peeled and eaten together the night before.

There was no more talk of love or of romance or of metaphors, though this seemed to be a good thing, not bad. My parents talked more, I would say, and kissed less, and this seemed to make both of them happy, though I cannot say why.

We spent less time on the beach and more time in the car, driving, driving, driving along the Gulf of Mexico.

Daddy said, "Symbol City is a funny name for a town."

Mama said, "Mississippi was never a subtle state."

Daddy said, "It's funny how you end up somewhere, and then that's your life."

Mama said, "I guess."

Daddy said, "I think I would like to read more books. I used to always be reading a book when I was in the army."

Mama said, "I guess."

Daddy said, "I met this guy who was writing a book. He was a writer, that's what he told me."

Mama said, "Is that right? I heard John Dillinger the gangster used to drive down this very highway."

Daddy said, "What has that got to do with a writer?"

We were in the car with the windows down. I was in the backseat thinking about cocksuckers.

I said, "Daddy."

Daddy said, "What is it, Sugar-man?" Then he said, "I could have given this writer a few tips for his book, if I'd of thought of it."

Mama said, "Tell the truth."

I said, "What if I wanted to grow up to be a cocksucker?"

Daddy said, "Sex facts about animals, that's what the book was about, see. He was collecting sex facts about animals."

Mama said, "I know one. I know a good one."

Daddy said, "You do? You know a good sex fact about animals?"

Mama said, "The common opossum has a forked penis. That's one, that's the one sex fact about animals that I know."

I got real quiet in the backseat. I had never heard my mother talk about sex before. It was stranger than seeing the silk ties on the bed posts.

Daddy said, "A *forked* one?"

Mama said, "That's it."

Daddy said, "Woo-ee."

Mama said, "In case they want to boink up the nose, I guess, I don't know."

The two of them laughed quietly at the joke. The wind was whipping through the car and stirring up dust devils in the backseat. The Gulf skies were blue, blue. It would have been an excellent time to be sitting on a hardwood floor instead of in the backseat of a car, I was thinking.

We drove along for a while and didn't talk.

Daddy said, "In the army I was stationed in Sarasota for a while." He said, "Friend of mine was with the circus. He was a swordswallower."

He seemed to be talking to me. I wondered if this was an answer to my question about cocksucking.

I said, "The circus?"

He said, "The winter circus. It's in Venice, near Sarasota. If we had an extra day or two we could drive down there. I wonder if he's still alive. He could take eighteen inches right down his throat."

Mama said, "It's so far to Sarasota, honey, and we're so comfortable here."

Daddy said, "Okay, all right, it was just a thought." He looked at Mama. He scrunched down in the driver's seat and looked through the steering wheel at the highway. He said, "I'm John Dillinger, rolling through, balling the jack, watch out, po-lice, watch out law-abiding citizens, watch out all you possums and cocksuckers!"

She said, "You're John Dillinger all right. You *think* you're John Dillinger." My mama was blushing and laughing, and she was flushed with excitement and joy.

He said, "You're my moll, bebby. You're a dangerous woman. You're the Lady in Red. You're my pistol-packing mama."

He gunned the engine and we sped along laughing like a bunch of wild Indians down the long bad coastal highway of the Gulf of Mexico.

Daddy said, "Git on down the damn road! Yeah!"

# Field and Stream

MY GIFT under the Christmas tree the year I turned twelve was a single-shot .410 gauge shotgun. It was a fine-looking little gun, with a dark-wood stock and forepiece. It breeched with a sharp metallic crack, so that a shell might be dropped into the chamber.

The shells were another gift, a bright box of number six shot. And also a canvas hunting jacket with a game bag built into the lining, and a canvas cap as well, with earflaps that could be pulled down in case of cold weather. Next to these was a stiff bright pair of wool boot socks, gray with a red stripe around the tops.

Not only were these things under the tree, which would have made my life complete in any case, but also a small sturdy metal box with two suitcaselike latches. I flipped open the latches and saw what was almost too good to be true, a sectional ramrod, a bottle of cleaning solvent, patches of cotton swabbing and a length of soft cotton rope. Also, a can of gun oil, a bottle of something called "blueing," and a thin pamphlet titled "Care and Cleaning of Firearms."

It was just daylight Christmas morning. My father was puking in the bathroom from drinking too much the night before. The fat red Christmas tree lights were shining and there was an angel on top of the tree. My grandfather was in his room smoking a cigar, though it was only six o'clock on a misty Mississippi morning, and the house stunk weirdly of tobacco and oranges.

I was holding the shotgun across my lap where I sat on the floor.

My mother said, "Do you like it?"

I said, "It's okay. Yeah, it's fine."

She said, "I wasn't sure it would be what you wanted. I was guessing. I hope I guessed right. Is a .410 all right? Is a .410 what you wanted?"

I said, "You can't hunt deer with it. It's too small for deer hunting."

My mother said, "Well, but maybe you wouldn't want to start with, you know, big game. Maybe you'll want to hunt, maybe, squirrels at first, until you're more experienced, maybe. Maybe rabbits."

I turned the gun on its side. I had to force myself not to pet it, like a living thing. I read the writing stamped into the barrel. *Winchester .410 gauge Full Choke*

I said, "Full choke."

My mother said, "Was full choke the wrong thing to get? Mr. Gibson at the Western Auto Store didn't mention anything about 'choke.' Or if he did, I mean, I guess I didn't hear, wasn't listening carefully. I don't even know what 'choke' means. Is full choke all right?"

We could hear my father finishing up in the bathroom. The big finish this morning, with the final gags of dry heaving and the scuffing sounds of his crawling on the floor, where he had been lying with his head in the toilet. Now the spitting and the cursing. Next the gargling.

Even my mother had to notice. She said, "Dad's driving the porcelain bus this morning."

I said, "'Modified' or 'open' choke would be better for quail."

She said, "But how about squirrels, or maybe rabbits? Just to start, you know, to get some experience first. Would full choke be all right for either of them?"

My mother was sitting on the floor beneath the Christmas tree with her hands in her lap. The fat red bulbs burned among the tinsel behind her. I cocked the hammer, and then eased the hammer back to the 'Safe' position. I sighted along the barrel, out the window at a pecan tree, black with rain from the night before.

I knew nothing at all about guns. This was the first gun I had ever held in my hands. I lowered it from my shoulder and did not look up.

I said, "Full choke is perfect for squirrels."

In my room, behind the closed door, I held the gun, I breeched it, and cocked the hammer. I even loaded it once, dropped a dangerous bright little plastic-coated cylinder into the chamber and snapped the gun shut and cocked the hammer and aimed from the hip at my closed door and knew that I could shoot right through it.

I took the gun apart, barrel and stock, and laid each piece on my bed separately. Then I put the parts back together.

I read *Field and Stream* magazine. I read about rifled slugs, about removing musk glands from animals, about cooking wild game, about constructing a dove blind in a harvested corn field. I read advertisements for insulated boots, for "pocket warmers," for battery-operated socks, for long underwear and waterproof shell bags. I looked at the men in the ads wearing flannel and leather and canvas and rubber. Men with pipes in their mouths and color in their faces.

And sometimes I even took the gun to bed with me, beneath the covers. I dumped the shells out of their box and scrambled them with my hand over the sheet, just to listen to the click. I picked them up and let them run through my fingers like gold.

THOUGH I did these things, I did not go hunting. With the exception of one aborted attempt soon after Christmas, my father resisted steadfastly all my mother's suggestions that he take me. Whenever the subject came up, he lapsed into sentimental memory. He told of a man who hunted with "a little beagle dog, sweetest baby voice you ever heard on a dog, like banjos far off in the woods somewhere," and when that poor man accidentally shot and killed that sweetest of animals one day, why, my father said, "He set down on the bumper of his truck and believe it or not because he was a big man, six foot ten or eleven, he set down on the front chrome bumper of his truck and he cried. I mean *cried like a baby*." He would tell this story several times in rapid succession, only varying the height of the crybaby on the bumper of the truck.

And yet, at night beneath the covers I fed a romance of nature and all its rhythms of forest and field.

For weeks my mother worked her small manipulations. "You know, there's nothing quite so beautiful to me as a father and son together," she might say at the dinner table. She might actually place her right hand on my father's shoulder and her left hand on mine and make a physical connection between us. Her words were the blessing and benediction that should have made the magic work.

Nothing did work, of course, hinting least of all. And not direct pleading. "Please take him, Gilbert. Take the boy hunting. Get to know him, you hardly know the child." This had as little effect as her subtler attempts.

Then one frozen Saturday morning in February, I woke up with both of my parents standing above my bed, my father saying, "Get up, Sugar, I'm taking you hunting."

My mother was actually wringing her hands. The wedding ring on her left hand, a simple thin gold band that fitted loosely beneath the knuckle, was for a moment the only thing of her that I could see, and it struck me to the heart with loneliness.

"Get up," my father was saying, harshly. "We're going hunting."

I rubbed my eyes and sat up against my pillows.

My mother said, "But will you be careful? You will be careful, won't you? Sugar, please be careful, listen to your father. Gilbert, teach him about safety. I'd just, I mean if anything happened to him, I'd just, just. . . ."

My mother and father had had a fight. It could have been about anything. This was his punishment of her.

My father took the canvas coat and cap from my closet and tossed them onto the bed beside me. He said, "Dress up like a hunter. Let's have a look at Mama's little hunter."

My mother wrung her hands and then picked at the frayed sleeve of her robe. She said, "Teach him safety, Gilbert. Please? Teach him all about safety."

He said, "You're the one wants him to go hunting."

To me he said, "Bring along that fine gun-cleaning kit too. You might need to clean your gun, you don't know. You never can tell when you might need a gun-cleaning kit along with you."

MY FATHER was wearing no hunting clothes, and he had no gun. He was wearing a pair of slick polyester pants, shiny as a lizard, and he had on a heavy corduroy coat and a pair of yellow plastic shoes, loafers of an unbelievable strangeness, that somebody had told him were the latest thing, and for which he had paid five dollars. It was difficult, in the presence of those plastic shoes, to keep on believing that I was a person who would ever resemble the men in *Field and Stream* who stirred fragrant pots of wild stew over campfires in the wilderness.

We left the house with my mother still wringing her hands and saying, in as cheerful a voice as she could invent from her despair, "Now you boys be careful, just be real extra careful, and, uh, and have yourselves a, uh, you know, good time." As we pulled away in the car, she called out, "Teach him firearm safety, Gilbert!"

As I've said, this was not the first time my father had set out with me to go hunting. The other time was a few days after Christmas, before the first of the year. Then he had said, "Hole up just a minute, Sugar, I'm thinking I might stop off at the Delta Cafe for a minute."

He was stopping to drink, of course. "You stay out in the car," he said. "I'm not going to be but one minute."

I stayed in the car for an hour. And then I took off my canvas jacket and hat and walked to the big plate-glass window and looked through the sign painted on it—I peered through the big hole in the D of Delta—and saw my father sitting on a stool at the counter with many other men. One of the men had a wicker basket full of newly born puppies. He must have been trying to give them away, to find homes for them.

Then I saw my father take one of the pups from the wicker basket and rub its little head with his forefinger. He held the pup up to his face and seemed to be talking to it, sweetly I thought, and then he talked to the man with the basket in his lap. My father drank a shot of whiskey and made his face, like oh yes! and then took a sip of beer behind the whiskey. Then he did the most remarkable thing I had ever seen anyone do.

He turned the puppy around and took the dog's tail in his mouth, between his teeth, and bit the dog's tail off, clean off, and spat it onto the linoleum floor, under a table where a couple was eating catfish. I could hear no sound, but the puppy was obviously squealing with surprise and pain.

There was blood all over the front of my father's shirt and on his chin. He was grinning proudly, as if he had done something fine. When the dog's owner had recovered himself—it took only a second or two—he took the pup from my father and looked at the other astonished faces sitting behind beers at the counter and said not a word. The expression of complete disgust for my father was sufficient. No words were necessary. He wrapped the puppy's tail in a napkin and picked up the rest of the pups, in the basket, and turned to leave the café. I wanted to run, but I stayed there and watched the man come out the door.

As the door opened I could hear my father's voice. He said, "Put a little salt on that nubbin to help it heal!"

SO IT IS miraculous that for even one second I had been deceived by the romance of this possibility of a hunting trip.

Mr. Shanker was the pharmacist. This time my father and I were not stopping at the Delta Cafe for shots and beers. We were stopping at the drug store for opium. My father said paregoric was good for a hangover if you didn't mind the constipation. And to be helpful he sometimes gave Mr. Shanker an injection of morphine to help him sleep. Mr. Shanker was the only man in town to whom my father seemed sober in comparison.

Immediately now I received a clear picture of how the two of us looked, my father and I. We were clowns. He was wearing yellow plastic shoes and lizardly pants, and I was wearing stiff new canvas clothing several sizes too large for me, and the new leather of my unoiled boots was almost as yellow as my father's. My feet hurt like torture.

I was paralyzed by shame for the two of us. I was my father's son, there was no doubt in my mind, and it was impossible for me to tell which of us was more worthy of loathing and disdain. In addition to my preposterous outfit, I was carrying a shotgun and a metal box with the words *Gun Cleaning Kit* stenciled on the front. "Don't forget your hunting equipment," my father insisted in his ironic way when I tried to leave the gun and kit behind in the car.

I followed my father through the front door of the drug store and breathed in the strange chemical fragrance that hung forever in its unholy air.

There was no one in the drug store.

My father called out, "Shank!"

There was no answer. Mr. Shanker was rarely conscious.

Again, he said, "Shank, where are you, boy?" He said this in his ironic voice, and then looked at me and gave me a sharp wink.

I felt loaded down with clothing and the shotgun and the gun-cleaning kit. There was a long soda fountain with a marble top, and a long mirror behind the counter.

In the reflection I could see clearly the shelves of things behind me, the tonics and patent medicines and mustard plasters and bunion pads and suppositories and boxes of Kotex, all the bright primary colors of their bottles and boxes and packaging. I could see a glass counter where Mr. Shanker had placed costume jewelry for sale, large gold-looking earrings and necklaces, impressive large bottles of perfume with French words in the name and glass stoppers as big as the bottles themselves, bud vases and ceramic masks and even chocolates in gold foil, stale for a decade.

But I could not see myself. I could not bear to look. I could not permit reality to swamp the invention and romance of

*Field and Stream.* I looked in the mirror and saw the drug store, but I could not, would not see myself.

Mr. Shanker was in the back room, my father told me.

Still carrying the .410 and the gun-cleaning kit and with a loose box of shells click-clacking in my jacket pocket, I followed my father through the large silent old barn of a pharmacy, with its perpetual chemistry and perpetual twilight and antique soda bar.

Mr. Shanker was in the back room all right. He was not dead yet, but he soon would be. He was filthy and soaked in his own urine and lying on an army cot beneath a wool army blanket. He was shivering so hard I thought he would fall right off the cot and onto the floor. The room was narrow and high-ceilinged and cramped and black-dark, and everything I needed to know of it I could smell or hear, the piss and the rattling of the cot against the floor, the rattling of something else, something inside Mr. Shanker, some clatter in his chest.

My father groped around above his head in the darkness and finally laid a hand on a string hanging from the ceiling. An enormous light bulb flashed on and filled the cavelike room with harsh light.

Mr. Shanker's eyes looked like a busted-out windshield. His face was an incredible orange color in the glare of the electric bulb. He was literally bouncing on the cot, his shivering was so extreme. The smell of his urine was strong.

Even so, Mr. Shanker made the last joke of his life. He said,

"Gilbert, they won't no need for the boy to shoot me. Those yaller shoes of yours'll do the trick by theyself." When he finished saying this, he opened his mouth and his enormous blue tongue rolled out like a snake. There was no sound, but I understood this to be laughter.

My father said, "Look like you bout to need a pick-me-up."

Mr. Shanker finished his weird tongue-laughter and motioned with his eyes to the syringe and morphine in a small black leather case on a low table nearby. The tongue sucked back into Mr. Shanker's mouth like a blue runner into a hole.

I said, "Daddy, he's dying."

My father said, "Lemme see that kit." He meant the gun-cleaning kit I was holding in my arms like a baby.

Mr. Shanker had swallowed his tongue and was choking to death.

I was rigid with fear.

My father said, "Gimme that goddamn kit, Sugar, you want to kill Mr. Shanker or what!"

I shoved the metal box toward my father and he took it in his hands. He set it on the low table and snapped open the latches. He said, "Now ain't that just the way the Lord his mighty works doth perform?" He was saying what a fortunate thing we had this gun-cleaning kit along with us, just at a time when Mr. Shanker was swallowing his tongue. My father was in a spiritual mood.

My father stripped the shortest section of the ramrod loose from the velvet-lined box and jammed it between the choking man's teeth and pried open Mr. Shanker's mouth. He said, "Hand me that box of swipes." He meant the package of cleaning swabs that normally fit at the end of the ramrod to clean gunpowder residue from a barrel.

Now he had Mr. Shanker's mouth open, with one section of the ramrod cracking the enamel off Mr. Shanker's teeth and his fingers down Mr. Shanker's gullet groping around for his tongue. The cleaning swab between my father's fingers gave him a good grip on the slick tongue, and so it was not long before he had grabbed hold of it and pulled it up to the surface like a fish. Mr. Shanker was actually breathing again.

My father was competent and calm and in control of the situation. For a moment I felt almost good about my life, I felt less lonely and more hopeful than I had for a long time. Mr. Shanker's tongue was as big as a bullfrog, and while it was no longer hopping, it did seem to have a life of its own, and to breathe in a healthy, regular rhythm, unlike Mr. Shanker's own real breathing.

My father said, "Hole on to this thang for a minute, Sugar."

He meant the tongue. He meant Mr. Shanker's unbelievable reptilian tongue.

I said, "I cain't do it, Daddy."

He said, "Shore now. Jess put down your mighty weapon there and grab holt of it."

Mr. Shanker's eyes were popped out and throbbing with blood and jaundice.

I leaned the .410 against the wretched army cot and moved into position behind my father. He set the gun-cleaning kit carefully on the cot beside the shotgun.

He said, "Use that-air swipe. You can get a better grip."

I said, "I don't think I can do it, Daddy." I took a cleaning swab between my fingers and reached around for Mr. Shanker's tongue.

My father said, "Have you got it?"

I was holding the tongue on one side and my father still had a grip on the end of it.

He said, "Okay, I'm letting go."

I said, "You're letting it go? You're letting it go right now?"

He said, "Have you got a-holt of it? Are you ready?"

I said, "I got it. I think I've got it."

He said, "All right then, I'm doing it, I'm letting go."

My father let go, and I held on like a bulldog. I had Mr. Shanker's tongue by the balls. This tongue was going nowhere. We had passed the baton.

My father said, "Good, good. Good work, Sugar-man."

I stood there holding the tongue while my father prepared the shot of morphine. Mr. Shanker's tongue was as passive as a fed cat.

It was almost like hunting. It was almost like *Field and*

*Stream.* The great strange electrical bulb swinging from a cord above us was the blazing Mississippi sun, it was corn fields and sorghum and sugar cane, it was a campfire in the woodlands, it was a lantern to skin squirrels by, it was the harvest moon to sleep beneath, it was the Milky Way and all the stars above, it was electrical socks and a brier pipe and chocolatey tobacco, it was father and son together in a place so primitive that age and old hatred and all of history made no difference, it was love and bright water and dark wood.

My father filled the syringe and found an uncollapsed vein in Mr. Shanker's skeletal arm, and swabbed the vein with cleaning solvent, and tied a tourniquet from the small coil of soft cotton rope.

He said, "Keep a hold on that tongue," and I tightened my grip so hard that I pinched a blood blister into it with my fingers.

THERE IS not much way to tell the next part except just to go on and tell it.

My father inserted the needle in the vein of Mr. Shanker's bruised and filthy arm, and pumped the little handle of the syringe, and filled Mr. Shanker's blood with morphine, and killed him dead.

There was a brief seizure and a few seconds of jerkiness, and maybe even a little vomit, but not much. It was a sudden death, if you look at it the right way. Mr. Shanker was dead of an overdose of morphine that my father administered thirty seconds after saving his life from suffocation by tongue.

My father said, "Some days I swear to God it don't pay to get out of the damn bed."

WHAT HAPPENED next is a strange and marvelous thing.

There was nothing to be done for Mr. Shanker. He was dead. I don't know what I expected my father to do, or say. I had never seen a dead person before, though I suppose my father had.

My father sat down slowly on the edge of the cot beside Mr. Shanker. The electric light bulb overhead still cast its odd harsh light over everything, the filthy cot, the army blanket, the table, the drugs and crumpled clothing on the floor.

My father said, "I'll have to call Big Boy." He meant Mr. Chisholm, the town marshall.

I said, "Are we in trouble?"

He said, "No, Sugar. We're not in any trouble. Shank wouldn't want me to say I killed him."

I said, "We just found Mr. Shanker here like this?"

He said, "I'll work this all out with Big Boy. Don't you worry, Sugar-man."

My father kept on sitting there. He patted Mr. Shanker once on the knee, and then sat a little longer.

At first I didn't move, and then I started to pick up the bits and pieces of my gun-cleaning kit and put them away, the tip section of the ramrod, with Mr. Shanker's spit and tooth enamel still on it, the solvent my father had used to sterilize Mr. Shanker's arm, the used swabs, the cotton rope. All of it I fitted carefully back into the velvet-lined box, and then I snapped shut the latches.

For a little while neither of us spoke.

My father said, "I look like a fucking fool in these shoes."

It is hard to say why, but I am certain that this was the closest moment my father and I had ever shared. I was very much in love with my father, though I might have known even in this moment that something inside me had frozen solid and would be a long time in thawing.

I said, "Is the hunting trip, you know, is it off again?"

My father rubbed his unshaven face with both his hands.

He said, "Do you still want to go hunting?"

I said, "Well, I wouldn't mind. Sure. Okay."

He said, "You're not just saying this? You really want to?"

I said, "Well, you know—if you want to."

He shook his head. He said, "Tell you the truth, if I was a fine boy like you I wouldn't much want to go hunting with a man like me."

He put his hands in his lap and studied the backs of them.

I said, "You mean a murderer?"

He looked up. He said, "Oh, well yeah, that too. I was more thinking about, you know, these damn shoes. Going hunting with somebody wearing yellow plastic shoes."

I sat down on the cot beside my father and the late Mr. Shanker. I could feel the warmth of my father's arm against my arm, and the warmth of Mr. Shanker's dead body against my butt and lower back. I leaned comfortably into the corpse.

My father said, "Do you really think I'm a murderer?"

I said, "I don't know." I said, "But you could throw the shoes away. That's something you could do."

My father said, "You're right there. I could do that. I could get rid of these damn shoes."

My father slipped off one shoe, very slow, and held it a moment and then dropped it into Mr. Shanker's paraphernalia-cluttered wastebasket. Then with the other shoe he did the same. He crossed his legs and rubbed his foot with his hands.

He said, "They wont even comfortable."

Mr. Shanker was very warm. I wondered how long it took for a body to grow cold.

I said, "You could cry like a baby."

My father said, "I couldn't do that, Sugar-man. Oh-no, I don't think I could do that."

I said, "I guess not."

I thought of my father's father, the bitter old man back at

the house. What did he have to do with this strange moment in my family's history? I could smell cigars and oranges.

I said, "I've never fired a gun."

My father said, "Well, you're right. You're right about that. And that's another thing we can do something about."

He stood up and took the gun and the gun-cleaning kit out of my hands.

He said, "Here you go, let me carry these for a while."

I handed everything over to him.

He said, "I think we'd better find me some decent shoes and call Big Boy Chisholm and figure out some way for me and you to burn some gunpowder before this day turns out to be a total loss."

# PART III

# How Bob Steele Broke
# My Father's Heart

NAUGHTY DEMONS accompanied my father wherever he went. All misery did not seem to be of his own making. In his home, the telephone often rang with no one on the line. Hoses broke on the Maytag. Pipes froze in the spring. Pets came down with diseases they had been inoculated against. Wrestling and "The Love Boat" appeared on television at unscheduled times. Lightning struck our house and sent a fireball across the floor. He was the only man in Mississippi to buy a bottle of Tylenol that actually had a cyanide capsule in it. He went to only two high school baseball games in his life and was beaned by a foul ball at each of them. A homeless person died on his back stoop. When he walked down the street bluejays chased after him and pecked at his face. He was allergic to the dye in his underwear. He mistakenly accepted a collect obscene phone call.

This sounds like a joke or an exaggeration, but I swear it is not. There was something magical about the amount of benign bad luck that, on a daily basis, swept through my father's life like weather and judgment.

After the separation my mother was suspicious of the outcome of any reunion with my father. He had quit drinking, it was true. And I was home on furlough from the army to lend her moral support, that was true as well. But even if she could have forgiven the incident with the knife, there was some chance, at least, that a reconciliation could lead to busted plumbing or bad wiring.

I should say more about the incident with the knife.

A year earlier, just before I went into the army, my parents had one of their usual fights.

My mother: "You, you, you!"

My father: "But, but, but . . ."

My mother: "You never, you always!"

My father: "But, but, but . . ."

My father was drunk, of course. I went upstairs to hide, as I always did.

I turned on my father's small black-and-white television and watched part of a "National Geographic Special" about whales. Japanese whalers shot harpoons into whales and the whales dragged boatloads of people in raingear through bloody water. A cartoon special was scheduled, but the whales came on instead. My father's portable television set.

Later wrestling came on, though "The Cowboy Bob Steele Film Festival" was scheduled.

The fight was over, so that was good.

I got out of bed and started downstairs to take a leak.

I walked past the kitchen just in time to see my father take a butcher knife from the sink and stab himself in the stomach.

He was wearing only a light cotton robe, which was open in front. My mother had already gone to bed.

Then he stabbed himself again, and this time the knife sank two or three inches into his stomach.

For a second I was stone, and then I said, "Daddy!" and rushed to hold him in case he should fall. I said, "Oh my God! Oh Jesus, Daddy!" I had my hands on his shoulders, and I tried to lead him to the sofa.

He drew the knife out of his stomach and dropped it on the kitchen table. Blood spilled down out of him, down his belly, down into the hair between his legs, down his thighs, onto the floor.

All I could say was, "Oh Jesus, oh Jesus."

My father said, "Hand me one of those cup towels from the rack. Watch that rack don't fall off the wall."

He took a clean dish towel and held it against the wound. I said, "I'll wake Mama."

He said, "Don't do that, Sugar. She's had a rough night. Let the pore woman get some sleep."

I said, "I'll drive you, then." To the hospital, I meant.

He said, "Well, but somebody's going to have to clean up this mess."

So that was that. I stayed behind to wipe up the blood with a sponge and wash it down the kitchen sink.

I heard the car start up in the driveway—it was a Pinto he

had bought from Runt Conroy, my friend Roy Dale Conroy's daddy, the car that later would actually explode, but tonight it started on the first try and there was no fire. I saw the lights come on, and then I watched out the window as my father backed the car out and drove up the street towards the highway and on to the hospital in Leflore, ten miles across the Delta.

After this incident my mother had had enough. She told him he would have to leave.

He said, "I'm going to make this up to you. I'm going to become a new man, you wait and see. I'm going to change my luck."

It was when I was on leave from the army, sometime in the spring of the following year, that my father came back to our house to beg to be taken back. That's what I thought he had come to do, anyway.

It was hard to deny that he was different. He had stopped drinking, for one thing. He went to meetings that he called his Don't Drink meetings, and to tell the truth, I had never seen him more in the flush of good health. It had been almost a whole year since he had a drink.

I had a brand new stripe on my dress greens and a spit shine on my shoes, and my mother seemed more at ease with herself than I had ever known her to be. Now here was my father going to his meetings and saying he might have his teeth fixed.

So when my father told me in confidence that he was planning to ask my mother's forgiveness for all his years of drunkenness, well, it didn't seem impossible to me that something very good might come of it.

My mother was not completely unaware of what might be in the offing. My father had called her and had asked, in his gentlest way, to be allowed to speak with her about matters of a personal nature. He said he was working a "step" of some kind for his D.D. meetings and would appreciate my mother's cooperation. This was the way he phrased his request, and so in my mother's mind it could mean nothing else except that he wanted to be taken back.

I need not go into the details of why she might oppose a complete reunion. Her life was moving along well enough, she had adapted to the small town gossip about the separation and the suicide attempt and my father's embarrassing Don't Drink meetings. She must still have harbored some grudge about the final scene at the house, the stabbing.

But in fact there was an irresistible quality about my father's particular doom. It did not seem entirely related to alcoholism. It seemed more cosmic, as if there were demons other than rum that did not care for my father at all.

The appointed day and hour arrived. I was home on leave, as I said. "You'll want to talk privately," I said to my mother, in an effort to get away from the house.

My mother insisted that I stay. "I need you here," she said. "If he asks to come back I'll need you here beside me."

I said, "What will you say?"

She said, "I'll say no. If he says, 'I'm sorry,' I'll say, 'I forgive you.' If he says, 'Take me back,' I'll say, 'No, I can't, it's too dangerous.' But you have to be here. If you are not here I might say yes."

So we waited for him.

My mother said, "I'll straighten up the kitchen."

She straightened it up, she more than straightened it up. She mopped the floor, she unloaded the dishwasher, she put new dishtowels on the rack, she scrubbed the sink, she put Drano in the pipes, she scoured the range and sprayed the oven with Oven Off, she cleaned the venetian blinds and swept a cloth-covered broom over the cobwebs in the ceiling corners.

She said, "Do you know how to put up wallpaper?"

I said, "Mama, he'll be here soon."

She said, "I didn't mean I'd hang the paper right this minute!"

I said, "Why on earth would you say yes?" I wanted her to say yes.

She took off her rubber gloves and sat in a kitchen chair. She mopped sweat off her forehead with the back of her forearm.

She said, "He's just so helpless, Sugar. When all those bad things happen to him, I just can't keep from wanting to help him."

I said, "But do you love him?"

She said, "I don't even ask myself that question any more. It doesn't even matter any more."

At last my father's car appeared in front of the house. It was the Pinto. The car was just out of the shop for electrical and fuel pump problems, as usual. My father did not seem to mind paying large sums to have the car repaired. He expected mechanical failure.

Here is what I know now. When he came to the house on this day, my father had no intention of talking my mother into taking him back. His only purpose in coming was to say to my mother, "I have treated you badly. I am so very sorry."

My mother and I watched him out the front window. He sat for a few moments in his car. I thought his doors might have become accidentally locked, but I looked more closely and saw that his eyes were closed and his lips were moving. I think my father might have been saying a prayer. I think he might have been praying, "Keep the demons away from me while I do this thing." Who knows what he might have been doing. The key was probably stuck in the ignition, or the seat belt would not come unbuckled.

My mother said, "Jesus!" as if he had just done something awkward or unusual.

I said, "Poor Dad."

She said, "Oh, poor Dad, my foot! I am so sick and tired of hearing Poor Dad!"

The door opened and my father stepped out of the car. For a moment he stood beside the car and mopped his forehead with his handkerchief. He also seemed to be sniffing the air. Testing the air, maybe. For a fragrance of spring flowers? For a fragrance of fresh paint from a back-yard fence nearby? For the ripeness of possibilities, or something to do with his car, maybe, a flooded carburetor? It was impossible to tell.

My mother said, "What is that fool doing now?"

I said, "Mama, it hurts me for you to talk like that. He's not doing anything."

She said, "He's bringing his bad luck with him. He's going to infect me with his bad luck again."

I said, "You are in love with him. That's why you're so scared of him."

She said, "I'm not letting him move back into this house. He can have a minute to talk, but that's all. That's all he's going to get from me."

My mother opened the door and allowed my father to come into the living room.

She said, "You might as well sit down."

My father eased himself down onto the sofa, where he had once accidentally sat on the cat and broken its neck. He was careful to sit on nothing but cushions.

My mother said, "Sugar, you sit down too."

I sat on the other end of the sofa and made myself otherwise invisible. I looked steadfastly out the window and except for polite greetings said nothing.

My father was not an articulate man. He scarcely noticed my presence. His face was pinched with concern for what he was about to say. *I'm sorry.* That's all he meant. I was beginning to understand that now. All he would have to do was say this and be gone.

Now my mother sat down as well. She was in the bentwood rocker. Not rocking but perched there, fragile as a bird on a twig.

This was it. My father was here to make amends.

Nothing happened. My father sat for a very long time and did not speak. His face was moving, his eyes, his jaw muscles, his ears and nose. There was even a wormy movement of his lips. He may have been speaking in there somewhere, he may have been carrying on conversations far back there in the silence. We didn't know. All my mother or I could know was that he was not speaking in the world in which we lived. He seemed to be carrying on a conversation in some other realm, where only he and the demons resided.

My mother kept waiting. Nothing happened.

My father put his hands on his knees. This may have been a gesture of decisiveness, it was hard to tell.

Some of my mother's anger had faded, or been stuffed out of sight somewhere. She was trying to help my father speak. "Can I come back, will you have me?" she believed he was trying to say from his weird silence.

She leaned forward in the rocker, as if to encourage him.

Still he said nothing.

My mother looked at me for help in jarring loose the words.

I offered nothing. I fixed my eyes on the tree outside our front window.

My mother looked back at him. Truly demons inhabited whatever space he occupied.

I wanted to say it for him. *I'm sorry. I didn't mean to hurt you.*

My mother wanted to say it for him. *Take me back. I can't live without you.*

Nothing.

My mother said, "Was there something you came to tell me, Gilbert?"

My father was sweating now. He wiped sweat from his face with the back of his arm. Then, immediately, he wiped his face with the other arm. His underarms were big full moons of sweat stains.

I thought, If he could have a drink of whiskey he could do this. Sobriety has killed this moment, this marriage.

My mother said, "Gilbert?"

He said, "Yes, please, thank you. I wonder if you could, if you might—I wonder if you would please give me a drink."

My mother said, "A drink?"

He said, "Tap water is fine, yes."

She said, "Water?"

I was already out of my seat. I filled a glass with ice cubes and ran water into it from the tap.

He drank the water and crunched up all the ice cubes.

He said, "There were eight of us."

My mother sat back in her chair, and allowed it to rock slightly for the first time since my father arrived in the house.

My father was talking about his own poor family in Canada. His brothers and sisters, his parents. He told about his father, who was blinded in the mines by coal dust.

My mother was very irritated now. She said, "Your father was not blinded by coal dust. Your father had cancer of the eyes."

He said, "Six children. Guided through life by a blind man and a crazy woman. Dishes were forever piled up in the blackened sink. My mother was odd. Now you would say she was depressed. Then she was only odd. Some days she couldn't move out of her chair. The table was never cleared. The oilcloth was stained with congealed foods. My father couldn't see it anyway, he was blind, but I could see it."

My mother said, "Gilbert, will you please get to the point?"

He said, "There was no telling what you might find on the breakfast table."

My mother had had enough. She said, "Gilbert, thank you for coming over."

He did not stop. He said, "A shoe, dirty clothing . . ."

Mother said to me, "Sugar, will you please . . ."

Father said, "A dead cat, once. Can you imagine that? A dead cat on the breakfast table."

Mother said, "I can imagine it all too well."

He said, "It was frozen, for some reason. Honestly, I can't think why."

She said, "I don't know what to say."

He said, "All I mean is . . ."

It was then that I heard the first sound. It was a sound like *wump*.

My father did not seem to hear the sound, but he did not finish his sentence either.

It was odd that he could not tell my mother he was sorry for their sadness together. He had apologized a million times in his life. On this occasion, though, when I suppose his words were genuinely important for the first time ever, he could say not a word that made sense.

Then the second time, this sound. *wump*. Small, distant, unreal. A cozy sound, I would say.

I continued to look out the window at the magnolia tree, as my father sat mute before my mother and me. My mother, in her anger, seemed to soften to the hope of hearing something sensible come out of my father's mouth. If he could have said, "I am sorry," she would have said, "I forgive you," and she would have meant it. If he had said, "I love you," she would have said, "I have always loved you," and this would have been true as well.

Out the window I saw the trees coming into leaf. Pecan and chinaberry and black walnut. I thought that those leaf-buds were almost voices. I thought that those new leaves, gold-green, were almost words, almost something being said. I believed, in this family silence, that I could hear the voices of the leaf-buds as a sound of their new growth. They were not just poised there, I watched them relax and spread. I believed that their greenness was a kind of grief.

My father said, "We ate cold canned spaghetti, dates, Post Toasties, Ovaltine, candy bars, soda water with cocaine in it, condensed milk by the teaspoonful. The contents of over-stuffed drawers hung down to the floor like sad cold animals."

My mother moved from her chair and sat on the floor by my father's feet and held his hand as he talked.

I was embarrassed. I stood and walked to the window and looked out.

He said, "I hated my pap for going blind. He beat me and my sisters. He tore us up as fine as cat hair."

Mother said, "I know, baby, I know."

Now that I was at the window and could see the street I knew what the sound outside had been. Hearthlike, had been one of my thoughts when I first heard this cozy sound. My father's car had exploded and was burning in full flame. There was a third sound of *wump,* and now a crackling and a sound of air rushing and being sucked somewhere.

I said, "Dad, your car is on fire."

He said, "I'm not trying to make excuses."

She said, "I know, I know."

He said, "It might sound self-pitying."

She said, "No, baby, no it doesn't."

I said, "Uh, excuse me. Dad, your car is, you know, on fire."

He said, "My house gets robbed, my TV picks up programs that are no longer aired, people I don't know call me up on the telephone."

Mother said, "We never should have let that white cat sleep on a white couch in the first place."

I said, "I'll just call the fire department."

He said, "I'm just so sorry for everything. For the way things turned out."

She said, "Learn to love yourself, Gilbert. For once in your life, learn to love yourself."

We could hear the sirens now. The Arrow Catcher Volunteer Fire Department was on the move.

The Pinto looked like a forest fire. It would not be long before the gas tank blew and rocked the neighborhood. The black smoke from the tires looked like a tornado.

Now the three of us stood at the window together and watched the flames rise, and we were happy together when the Arrow Catcher pumper truck turned the corner at the Methodist church and banged to a halt in front of our house.

I wish this story ended more happily than it actually does. All this happened a long time ago, and now I'm middle-aged and have been going to Don't Drink meetings for a good long while myself. There is a good deal of wreckage in my own past, a family I hurt in the same way my father hurt me, and the same way his father hurt him. I tore my children up as fine as cat hair, you might say.

And I wish I could tell you that my father died a happy man, or at least a sober man. But the truth is he died a dozen years later underneath a blanket of fish. That, however, is another story. His skin was as yellow as a traffic light. These were hard times for all of us, especially for my mother.

But the night my father came over to the house and made amends to my mother and blew up his car, none of this sadness seemed possible. And for that blindness to the future I will always be grateful.

That night my father and my mother slept together in their bed in their house, for the first time since he stabbed himself. I imagine that she looked at the scar on his stomach for the first time ever. I imagine that she ran her fingers over it and maybe kissed it as a part of their love-making that night.

I heard nothing, not even their quiet voices, and not the sound of their touching. But I know this fantasy must be true, this dream of romance. There was such hope in all of us then.

Let me tell you what did happen that night. I was lying in the same bed, in the same room with the slanted ceiling and luminous decals of stars and planets above me, where I had lain on the night of the stabbing. The same magnolia tree scratched at my window. The same peach-basket-size moon celebrated the width of the Mississippi sky. I watched the same black-and-white television set that I had watched that night.

This night I did not follow a light in the kitchen and find my father there with a knife. This night my father left my mother asleep in their bed and eased inside the door of my room and stood without speaking with his back leaned against the door frame.

I said, "Hey, Daddy."

I was waiting through a commercial for the beginning of "Petticoat Junction." I met a boy in the army who had been to Hollywood and had walked through Petticoat Junction and Mayberry and two islands, Gilligan's and Fantasy. Because of him I tried to watch these re-runs whenever they were listed in *TV Guide*.

But when the commercial was over "Petticoat Junction" didn't come on. An old Western movie came on instead. It was a movie called *The Rider from Laredo,* with an actor named Bob Steele.

My father said, "Bob Steele." He was standing there, just inside my door.

I said, "*TV Guide* says 'Petticoat Junction' is supposed to come on now."

He said, "Bob Steele don't understand Western symbolism."

I said, "This television set is crazy. It never picks up what is supposed to be on."

He said, "He can't sing, either. Don't even try."

I said, "Bob Steele?"

We looked at the TV screen and watched a distant horse-back rider come into view. There was a dust cloud behind his horse.

My father said, "No wife, no white hat, no good-looking horse, no Indian sidekick, nothing."

The rider was close enough to see now. My father was right. There was nothing to distinguish this rider from a messenger, or a bad guy, or a minor character. There was no way to tell this was the star, the hero of the movie.

My father said, "And no comical sidekick either. Andy Clyde, Smiley Burnett—those guys wouldn't give Bob Steele the time of day."

We watched the movie. Bob Steele was not a good horse-back rider. The horse was a small brown nondescript beast that was jerking its head this way and that. Bob Steele was tired and hassled-looking from struggling with it. This was not part of the script.

There is a gunfight going on in town. Bob Steele finally cracks his horse over the head with his fist to make it settle down. He reins the creature to a halt and the horse's eyes are wild from fear of being punched out, blind-sided.

My father said, "Bob Steele don't take no shit from a horse."

It's a gunfight sure enough. On one side of the street are all the solid citizens, the ranchers and farmers and the parson and the church ladies in bonnets. On the other side of the street are the gamblers and the floozies and the real estate swindlers and the saloon guys in black hats.

My father said, "Watch this."

Bob Steele is not tall, is not handsome, has no bullwhip, or sidekick, no distinguishing features. He can't ride a horse, he can't sing. He is new in town, and what I begin to understand is that without any help at all, without even a white hat or an interesting horse, Bob Steele is pure gold. He is the believable de-symbolized, unromanticized version of what every man on earth wants to be. He is the magic that can be touched. He is what my father drank to become, and what I later drank to become. He is alone, he is pure hope, and complete.

Bob Steele jumps off his horse.

The two sides of the street are blazing away at each other. Men and women in violent conflict. Confined and victimized by their wardrobes, their unchangeable, unalterable representations of themselves and beyond themselves.

Bob Steele takes out his six-shooter and fires off several shots, first one way and then the other. The gun is smoking. And then Bob Steele speaks the first words of the movie.

He does not say, Stop in the name of the law. He is no lawman, no Texas Ranger. He does not say, Hold your fire, or I've got you covered. Here's what Bob Steele says. He says, "What's going on here?"

My father looked at me.

He said, "Do you see what I mean?"

I said, "I'm not sure. You mean, shoot first and ask questions later?"

My father said, "No, I mean ask the right question. Ask the same question over and over. Ask the only question there is."

I said, "Ask, 'What's going on here'?"

My father said, "Maybe, maybe that's the right question."

# Creatures with Shining Scales

THERE WAS rain all morning and the sky was as green as apples. It was only noon, and yet so dark the streetlights came on, right in the middle of the day.

My father had just died in the bedroom.

It was no surprise, he had been sick for a long time. My mother and I were sad, but also a little relieved.

The tornado was not one of those slender, graceful beauties that snake down from heaven to Kansas on the television news. This was a thick, black, squat barrel jutting down from a gunpowder-colored canopy above the swamp. An ugly Mississippi bullfrog of a tornado.

I had an excellent view of the storm from my father's room.

The rain was horizontal by now. I felt no fear of the window caving in and cutting me in two. I only stood there looking across our back yard, across the road.

My mother said, "Honestly, some days it does not pay to get out of bed."

I looked at my father's pale thin corpse in the bed and thought of covering his face with a sheet, but then decided not to. His eyes were closed, he looked all right, what was the point.

I looked out the window at the strange tablelike slab of rain in the air, gray as slate. A red coloring in the funnel—bricks, I finally realized—meant the county school was down. Or, actually, up—if you want to get technical about it. The bricks floated like weightless things. Great sheets of plywood sailed around the outside of the funnel and disappeared and then sailed back around again, like painted horses on the carousel. So houses were down as well, the new subdivision just beyond the swamp, I supposed.

A great noise issued from the sky. It was like a freight train, somebody was quoted as saying. A jet plane, somebody else said. To me it was a string of firecrackers going off, very fast but one at a time, sure enough, pop pop pop pop, a hundred reports one right after the other. A stand of one hundred loblolly pines snapped off, tree by tree.

My mother said, "Do you think we should take shelter?"

That was the first it occurred to me that our house would surely be hit. We were directly in the path of the storm.

I said, "Well, maybe so. Maybe that's a good idea."

My mother said, "I heard somewhere you could hide in the bathroom. The bathroom is supposed to be a safe place, for some unknown reason."

I said, "Well, all right. It sounds good to me. Let's get in the bathroom, maybe we'd better get moving."

We started to go into the bathroom, and then my mother stopped. She said, "What about your daddy?" His body, she meant, of course.

I said, "He's light as a twig. I could carry him into the bathroom with us."

The house was rocking now. Shingles were flying like pigeons.

She said, "You carried him to the bathroom often enough when he had to sit on the pot. You're a good boy, Sugar. You were always awfully good to your daddy and me. And not even your real daddy at that."

All the window screens blew off the house at once and flew away like large transparent birds.

I said, "Not my real daddy?"

She said, "You'd better get him. You'd better take him to the bathroom with us."

The house was cracking like a bullwhip. It felt like we were riding a snake.

The picture window was breathing in and out like a big-chested athlete.

I was already scooping the body up in my arms.

My mother changed her mind again. She said, "Put him down, Sugar. Come get in the bathroom. Don't do anything foolish, after you've been such a good son."

I said, "Are you sure?" I was holding my father's body in my arms like a sleeping child.

Water was pouring under the doors and heavy things were hitting the outside of the house. I put my father back down on his bed and went into the little interior bathroom with my mother and closed the door behind us.

Ten seconds later the storm was gone and so was the roof. Rain fell as if it were any other summer day, except that it fell into the house on us. Wet beards of Spanish moss draped from my mother's hair, sucked up out of the swamp and dropped here. There were pine cones in my lap. There were also heavy things, rafters with bright nails and roofing with dull-colored nails. There was a small cut above my right eye.

I said, "We don't know what we'll see when we dig ourselves out of here." Despite the wreckage of the house, and the wreckage of our lives, we could talk in more or less normal voices.

My mother said, "Maybe he blew away."

I said, "It's possible. In fact, he probably did blow away."

She said, "He was light as he could be. He didn't weigh any more than dandelion fluff."

I said, "I'll look. You stay here. I'll go out and look for him."

She said, "You have been such a good son to me. You have always been a good boy. Your daddy loved you so much, even if he wasn't your real daddy."

I said, "Uh, Mama . . ."

The bathtub was half filled with rainwater, and the rain continued to fall. We were stuck beneath debris, two-by-fours and shingles mostly, and many small fish that the storm had sucked up from the swamp and left behind in our bathroom and across the rugs and floors of our demolished house. Some were minnows, a million of them, small silvery creatures with shining scales. And there were larger fish as well, a small catfish or two, a gar with a snout.

My mother, there in the rain-filled bathtub, covered with debris, said, "I loved your daddy. For all his faults, I did love him."

I said, "Mother, do you remember the time Dad took me fishing and it made me so sad to see the fish die?"

She said, "Your daddy never took you fishing, Sugar. I begged him a hundred times to take you, but he never did."

I said, "No, I'm sure he took me once. He caught silvery-looking fish and I finally caught one, well, catfish I suppose, an ugly monstrous old creature of a fish. It looked nothing like the fish he was catching."

She said, "You must have dreamed it, Sugar-man. It never happened. Your daddy never took you fishing."

I dropped the subject and pushed away the last of the debris. I tested my legs and found that I could stand easily. I opened the bathroom door and went out into the house, though I might as easily have walked around the door frame.

The rain had slacked up now, in fact had almost stopped. The sky had lightened a great deal and, though I could see nothing but destruction everywhere, the day suddenly seemed to re-dawn, as if with some promise of good things rather than bad.

I could see through my walls. Neighbors wandered about in their yards, looking at the felled trees, the frames and shells of houses. I heard someone say something about a chainsaw.

My father had not blown away after all. He was still in his bed, as if asleep. There were many small fish in the bed with him. The sheets were silver and shimmering with fish going flippety-flip.

I said, "Mama, he's all right! He's still in bed. Daddy is just fine."

My mother said, "Well, I wouldn't go so far as to say that."

I said, "Mama, did you say—a while ago, did you say . . . ?"

I looked directly into my mother's face, and for the first time in my life I understood that she was a very beautiful woman, that many men had loved her, that her choices had been more varied and strange than I had ever imagined.

She said, "Did I say what, Sugar?"

# EPILOGUE

# Owls

ONCE WHEN I was a small boy of ten or eleven I was traveling late at night with my father on a narrow country road. I had been counting the number of beers he drank that night, nine or ten of them, and I was anxious about his driving.

Neither of us had spoken for a long time. What was there to say?—the beers, the narrow road, the stubble fields, a bare bulb shining out in the darkness from a porch far back from the road, the yellow headlights? What was there to talk about? The car held the road on the curves, the heater was making its familiar sound.

Then I saw a road sign, bright yellow and diamond-shaped, and on it I read the word SLOW. My father kept on driving at the same speed and did not slow down, though I knew he had seen the sign. So I was bold. I said, "Did you see that sign?"

Immediately my father let up on the gas and the car began to slow down. He said, "You're right. We should go back."

He pulled his car onto the berm and stopped and looked back over his left shoulder for safety and then pulled out onto the road again and made a U-turn.

I was frightened. I said, "Why are we going back?"

My father shifted the gears and we began driving back in

the direction we had come. "The sign," he said. "I'm going back to see the sign."

I said, "Why? Why are we doing that?"

He said, "Isn't that what you meant? Didn't you want to go back?"

I said, "I wanted you to slow down. I was afraid."

We drove on in the darkness for a minute. My father said, "The sign didn't say SLOW."

I said, "It didn't? I thought it said SLOW."

My father said, "It said OWLS."

So we kept driving and I didn't argue. I listened to the quiet sound of the heater fan. I saw the red eyes of a rabbit on the roadside. I saw the stubble fields. For one second I believed I had lived a very long hard life and that I was all alone in the world.

Then the sign came into view again, the back of the sign, of course. My father slowed the car and pulled over to the right and when he had come to a complete stop he checked over his shoulder for safety and made another U-turn so that we might face the sign again and read its message. The headlights made the sign huge and bright.

My father had been right. The sign said OWLS.

We kept sitting there for a long time. The engine was running, there was a small vibration.

Then my father turned off the engine. The early-spring night air was cold, but he rolled down the windows.

I knew my father wanted me to be quiet. I'm not sure how I knew this. I knew he wanted us to listen. I scarcely breathed I was listening so hard. I did not move at all.

Then I heard the owls overhead. I heard the soft centrifugal buffeting of their feathers on the night air. I heard a sound from their owl-throats so soft that I believed it was their breathing. In my mind I counted them and thought that they were many. The owls were circling and circling and circling in the air above us.

I don't know what I believed would happen. I think I believed I would feel the fingers of my father's hand touch my arm, the sleeve of my shirt. I believed I would turn to him and for the first time in my life I would know what to say. I would tell him all my secrets. I believed my father would say, "I love you." This was what it meant to sit in a car with your father in the middle of the night and listen to a flock of owls while looking at a diamond-shaped sign that said OWLS.

Then he rolled up his window, and so I rolled up mine. In the darkness he said, "You know, your mother is a terrible housekeeper."

We only sat there looking at the OWLS sign. I knew things would not go well after this.

And so then he started up the car and we drove away, back along the dark road, and we did not say anything else to each other that night, and he drank a few more beers.

All I mean to say is this: Many years later I fell in love with a woman, and she was beautiful and strange. One afternoon, after we had made our love, we lay in a band of sunlight that fell across our bed and I told her the story of my father and the dark road and the sign that said OWLS.

I said, "You don't believe me, do you?"

The woman said, "Have you ever told this story to anyone before?"

I said, "I told my mother. That same night, after my father and I got home and my mother came upstairs to tuck me in."

The woman said, "Tell me again about your room, then, with the fake stars on the ceiling."

I told her what she already knew. I said, "It was an attic room, with a slanted ceiling. A desk, and even my clothes drawers were built into the wall to save space. There was a crawlspace in the back of my closet, where I sat sometimes, in the rafters. On the ceiling above my bed were pasted luminous decals of stars and the planets and the moon. Saturn had rings. A comet had a funny tail.

She said, "Tell me again about the real moon."

I said, "The moon outside my window."

She said, "How large was it?"

I said what I had told her many times. I said, "It was a peach-basket-size moon."

She said, "And you were lying in your bed, with the fake stars shining down on you and the peach-basket moon outside your window, and then . . ."

I said, "I heard my mother coming up the stairs to tuck me in."

She said, "Your mother had been worried about you, out in the car with your father when he had been drinking."

I said, "Yes, she had been worried. She would never say this."

She said, "What did she say?"

I said, "She said, 'Did you have a nice time with Daddy tonight?'"

She said, "What did you say?"

I said, "I told her the story about seeing the sign. About stopping and listening to the owls in the air."

She said, "What did your mother say then?"

I said, "She said, 'That's about like your daddy.'"

She said, "Your mother didn't believe you?"

I said, "She was right. There was no OWLS sign. It's ridiculous. There is no way to hear owls in the air. And, anyway, think about the coincidence of a drunk man and his oversensitive kid stopping at just the moment the owls happen to be flying above a sign."

She said, "Hm."

I said, "And you know that thing my father said. That thing about 'Your mother is a terrible housekeeper'?"

She said, "Mm-hm."

I said, "That's a part of an old joke we used to hear in the South when I was a boy. The punchline is, 'My wife is a terrible housekeeper, every time I go to piss in the sink it's full of dirty dishes.'" I said, "I think I made the whole thing up."

She said, "Where did the owls come from?"

I said, "I'm not sure. Do you remember in Winnie-the-Pooh, the character named Owl?"

She said, "Yes."

I said, "Remember, somewhere, in one of those books, we learn that Owl's name is misspelled on a sign as WOL. Maybe that's where I got the idea. I just happened to think of that book. Jeeziz. It's possible I made this whole thing up."

She said, "Are rabbits' eyes really red?"

I said, "I don't know. I saw a blind dog in my headlights one time, and its eyes looked red. Christ."

The way the sunlight fell across the bed was . . . Well, I was so much in love.

She said, "Was your father magic?"

I said, "I wanted him to be."

She said, "He might have been."

Now she looked at me, and it was the night of the owls all over again. The car's heater, the vibration of the engine, the red eyes of the rabbit, the stubble fields, the music of the odd birds in flight, the OWLS sign before me. And also the feeling that there was someone beside me to whom I could tell my most terrible secret and that the secret would be heard and received as a gift. I believed my clumsy drunken inexpert father, or my invention of him, had prepared me for this magic. The woman beside me said, "I love you."

In that moment every good thing that I had expected, longed to feel with my father, I felt with her. And I also felt it with my father, and I heard his voice speak those words of love, though he was already a long time dead. He was with me in a way he could not be in life.

For one second the woman and I seemed to become twins, or closer than twins, the same person together. Maybe we said nothing. Maybe we only lay in the band of sunlight that fell across our bed. Or maybe together we said, "There is great pain in all love, but we don't care, it's worth it."

# Music of the Swamp

## The Invention of Sugar

*An Essay about Life in Fiction—and Vice Versa*

by Lewis Nordan

# The Invention of Sugar

*An Essay about Life in Fiction—and Vice Versa*

by Lewis Nordan

Once when I was a boy my father took me hunting with him. We were quail hunting on posted land, private property, and we had to cross through a barbed wire fence to enter a large field. There was a NO TRES-PASSING sign on the fence post where I leaned my single barrel shotgun while I held the wire down with my foot so that my father could sneak through. Then he held the wire for me.

With us we had a sorry, no-count yellow dog with a long tail and little sense of smell or direction, and none of responsibility. Throughout the morning the dog was worthless as a hunting companion. It raced through the stubble fields and scared off whatever quail might have been nearby, it chased rabbits, scratched fleas, humped our legs when there was a spare moment.

As hunters my father and I were as sorry as the dog. I did not look terrible—I was wearing blue jeans and a gabardine shirt and looked more like the schoolchild that I was than a hunter. My father looked worse. He was drunk and dirty and wore white painters' overalls, which he still had on after work, and on his feet wore a pair of yellow plastic shoes that somebody had told him were the latest thing and for which he had paid five dollars. My father kept shouting at the dog, "Got damn it, Blue! Got damn it!" Why my father should have named this sorry yellow dog Blue is anybody's guess.

I was honored to have been invited to come along with my father on a birdhunt, but I was also ashamed to be seen with him and this impossible dog. All my imaginings of woodland hunters came from *Field and Stream*, with its handsome caretakers of the wilderness, crisp canvas jackets, briar pipes, oiled leather, blued gun barrels and mahogany stocks.

I was consoled only that no one would have a chance to see and judge us, here in a field far back from the road.

And then that hope was dashed. Across the field my father and I spotted another party of hunters. These men might as well have stepped straight from the pages of *Field and Stream*. They were handsome men. Their shotguns were not the rusted-out single-shot Winchesters that my father and I carried. They were Browning automatics with gold inlay and engraved scenes of pheasants on the side. They had red rubber recoil pads on the gun butts and ribbed barrels. There were a dozen or more of these men. Their dogs were purebred retrievers, trained in St. Louis, holding points, backing up each other like statues until the hunters were in position to fire.

It was the governor of the state and all his party. The governor was a handsome elegant man, and I recognized him from the television news. The whole party of men were crack shots. A small covey of birds rose up in front of them and pop pop pop, the gunpowder burned and feathers flew and the bird carcasses dropped to the earth where gleaming dogs with mouths as soft as cotton picked them up and handed them over to the smiling gentlemen.

Our own dog, this yellow brain-damaged oversexed rabbit chaser that my father called Blue, was delighted to find that we had company. Blue raced over to the governor's party. He broke the points of the other dogs, the dismayed dogs, I should say, since these canine aristocrats had never actually known such creatures as Blue even existed. He tried to get up a rabbit chase, he humped a few legs, he nipped a few ankles, sniffed a few crotches, barked and got into a fight with a frightened puppy that seemed to be in training.

The governor and his party were tolerant honorable men, and for a time they were patient, but finally they were pushed beyond the point of human tolerance. When one of the hunters pushed Blue away with his foot—at this point Blue had hold of the man's pants leg and was snarling and yanking at the cloth—my father called the man a son of a bitch and threatened to sue him. "That's a valuable dog!" my father said. The governor had several dog-handlers with his party, decent black men who scurried here and there to corral their dogs and get them onto leashes before any real damage could be done. They avoided looking at me or my father, for I am sure they did not want to register either their disgust or their pity for us. It was impossible not to have recognized us for what we were, white trash to the core. I could scarcely breathe I was so frightened that my father would call one of them by an insulting racial epithet.

The governor himself turned away, so as not to have to speak with us, but other men in the party gave us firm advice, on the order of threats of legal action, that we were poaching on private property and if my father didn't want to spend a night in jail he would find somewhere else to hunt.

We left the woods and fields in disgrace, and—here is the punchline of the anecdote, and it proves that my father was not utterly disgraced— ever after this my father referred to the incident as "the day me and my boy went hunting with the governor."

I'VE TOLD THIS STORY many times over the years. It is a part of who I am, one of many deep important memories that have shaped my life. The thing is, though, not one word of the story I've just related is true. This is a deep important memory with no historical basis, you might say.

My father and I never went hunting together until I was grown and married, and then only once and it was squirrel hunting, not quail hunting, and with a lot of other people, not alone together. In fact, I never went quail hunting with anybody at all, let alone my father, and we never owned that yellow dog, though now, living in Pittsburgh, I have a dog that more or less fits this description. I never saw the governor of the state of Mississippi, except once when I went to Boys State in Jackson, and can assure you that he was neither handsome nor elegant nor tolerant and did not conform to any other description of him that I may have implied here. I once heard someone in Arkansas use the phrase "dogs trained in St. Louis" and so I adapted the phrase to my story (it's an intriguing phrase to me and worthy of a story, but why St. Louis, I have always wondered). I myself, and not my father, wore those yellow plastic shoes, but not on a hunting trip. I wore them off to college and was thrown in the duck pond at the Jackson zoo by my fraternity brothers as punishment for an unacceptable fashion statement (the shoes came off and sank to the bottom of the duck pond where I suppose they still lie, with the same approximate half-life as plutonium, these thirty-odd years later). My father never on earth would have considered suing anyone for anything, let alone making such assertions to strangers over a dog, nor would he ever have uttered a racial slur to anyone's face—all these things would have required his becoming visible to strangers. And if you should multiply all my father's wit and humor and capacity for self-directed irony by the number one million, he still never would have been capable of making an ironic judgment upon himself about "the day we went hunting with the governor." Nothing about this story ever happened. And finally to make an end of this lengthy point, the fact is, I never even knew my father. My father died when I was eighteen months old and my mother remarried when I was eight years old to a man whom I called Daddy and on whom all the fathers in my stories are based. He is my stepfather, actually. So my stepfather, not my natural father, is the man to whom none of what I've been writing applies.

THE ONE TRUE THING about this tale that I have just told is that I have been telling it as the truth for many years. Only recently, during a moment of honesty, or a lapse of what I'm learning to call "denial," did it occur to me that none of this had ever happened. I mean, I didn't decide after a long time to come clean, and stop all my miserable lying. I had not known that I was lying. I have told this story so many times and in so many forms that it is hard to believe myself right now as I tell you that it is not true. I mean, it isn't true, obviously, but it has been a part of my historical narrative for so long that it is in some senses more a true part of me than much of the stuff that actually did happen and that made little or no impression on me. (I am reminded of the Woody Allen line in which the comedian recalls a time when he started to drown and somebody else's whole life flashed before his eyes.)

I have now written three books in which I tell this story several times in one form or another. And from time to time I have believed that each of these renditions was somehow true, a part of my history and my life with father. Stepfather, of course.

In one story "my" father—the father of the child in the story—promises to take me to a carnival sideshow and then at the last minute he reneges and goes in alone to see the hermaphrodite. Goodbye, kid, go home, this is not for you, the father says in effect. In another he takes me camping and has no sleeping bags or lanterns or other equipment and I have to sleep under a picnic table in a park. In another he promises not once but twice to take me hunting and the first time gets drunk in the Delta Café and bites the tail off a dog and cancels the trip, and the next stops by the drug store for a few minutes and accidentally kills the pharmacist before we ever get to the woods. In another he and my mother are separated because of his alcoholism and when he comes over to make amends for all his wrong doing to her, he accidentally blows up his car. In another, an intimate moment between father and son, a game with the Sears Roebuck catalog seems actually to be the cause of the father's alcoholism and death. In another, in a magical moment in the

Mississippi wilderness when the child expects his father to tell him that he loves him, the father tells him instead that his mother is a terrible housekeeper. In another the father is incarnated as my blind grandfather and at just the moment when I have run away from home on a freight train and come near to despair and death and for once in my life have my mother's attention, he miraculously regains his sight and thereby grabs all the attention to himself and robs me of my moment of sympathy and glory. In another my father gives me a sex education lecture that requires locker room information to interpret.

There is a recurrent theme, and the structure is frequently the same. A child is set up to hope that one thing will be true and then the child's father is in power to interfere and cause the child to be disappointed. Ideal scenes are almost realized and then are snatched away. Let me be sure I am clear on this point: none of this ever happened to me. None of it. Not the train, the sex lecture, the explosive car, the dead pharmacist, the dog's tail, nothing. No doubt I suffered about the same number of disappointments as the next child but my stepfather never did any of these things to me, or in my presence.

So why do I keep saying that these things did happen? Why do I have a hard time distinguishing between what actually happened and what never happened—and not only in my written-down fiction but in my spoken memories of family life as well?

I'm not sure I know the answer to these questions, but I am sure that the pattern of romantic expectation and disappointment is pervasive in the stories I have written, and not only between fathers and sons. In one story a teenaged girl goes swimming with a beautiful man and fantasizes a romantic end to her ironclad virginity and ends up having to save the guy from drowning and relieve him of a scary phallic-looking lamprey eel that has somehow got attached to him. She comments on the reversal of her lifeguard fantasy—the fortunate weak, who should be saved, must unfairly become the strong. In another a child has a special secret, a bottle of kerosene hidden in his closet, from which he might make little fires on the lakebank for games of Indians, and to his horror his baby brother drinks the kerosene and dies. Another child with a secret, this time a small shovel, digs under his house, playing games of soldier, escaping prisoner, and gold miner, and unearths a corpse. In another a lovesick swain in college makes elaborate romantic plans to elope and at the crucial moment his wife-to-be oversleeps and he is made to look foolish in front of their friends. In another a husband, hoping to rekindle love and desire in his marriage, plans a romantic beach vacation, which ends in carnage and adultery and confirmation of the loss of hope and romance. In another a man in search of God and purity of love ends up exposing himself in a public place. In another no one comes to an elaborately planned birthday party.

So this apparently is what I have been blessed and cursed to write: the hope and expectation of intimacy and romance, and always their certain doom.

IT COULD BE SAID, I suppose, that this is the structure of all short fiction: somebody wants something, works hard against opposition to achieve it, until the striving for the goal reaches a crisis, and then, whether the original goal is achieved or not, the achievement can never be imagined again as simply or cleanly as it had been in the beginning of the story.

This is the theme of the anecdote with which I began, the story about my father's day in the field with the governor. A child wanted a *Field and Stream* life, he briefly occupied the stage with *Field and Stream* characters of the highest order, came away with strong confirmation of his own white trashery (which was the core of his need to fantasize such a life in the first place), and yet ends with a gentle memory of his father's silly irony that says, Well life's not so bad after all, even if we can't have what we want.

Put into these bald terms my story, and I suppose all fiction as I've described it here, seems hopelessly sappy—or, lacking the upbeat ending, merely hopeless, and so sappy for that reason as well.

But though these remarks might apply to fiction in general, and though I might make some justifying remarks about the hope of good writers being a discovery, over and over, of ways to tell this same story, or to repeat this same structure, an infinite number of times, and each time freshly and never reducible to its lowest form (or god forbid, formula!), I am really not so interested in fiction in general right now as I am in my own heart, my own particular, personal relation to this subject of the death of romance and the darkening of hope. It is this impulse in me that first caused Sugar Mecklin to draw breath.

So let me go back some distance, into my personal biography, and make some guesses about the meaning of my many inventions—short stories when they are written, damned lies when they are spoken as history to my friends.

When I was a baby my father died, so I am told. I have no memory of him, and only one photograph, in which he is holding me. I am dressed in a white gown, and he is wearing a hat that shades his eyes and also hides the one personal detail I have of how he looked, that he was bald—so I have very little of him to remember him by, not even a picture of his bald head. Whenever I think of my natural father he is always wearing a hat that covers his eyes. I own nothing that was his. None of his personal belongings and not even any anecdotes about him. In any case my earliest memories are of being the only child I knew whose father was dead.

For some time I believed that what I was writing out was simple anger at the man who took my mother away from me, my stepfather. I had my mother all alone until I was seven, I crawled into bed with her early on cold mornings, all our plans included only me. And then there he was in the bed with her. At night, from my own room down the hall, I could hear their lovemaking, and I covered my head with a pillow. On cold mornings when I was invited to snuggle with them in their bed, he was there, and unlike my mother's legs and feet, his were hard as nails. And then later there was his drinking and his silence, and his redneck drinking buddies, and his bad teeth and bad grammar, and my mother's crying, which he seemed responsible for. There is little doubt that I have been angry at him, and for rather conventional reasons.

It would be comfortable, and neatly Freudian, to continue to blame my stepfather for my belief in the disappointment of romance, and for all my obsession with interrupted, spoiled expectations. There is another part of this, though.

It was not simply that I didn't want this particular man to be my father. I had a father picked out for us, a different particular man, for my mother and me. I wanted my mother's brother to be my father, Uncle Bud. Uncle Bud was dashing and handsome, a physician who served in Africa with General Patton. He was outrageous and imaginative and garrulous, and at Christmas one year he wrapped his entire two-story house in tissue paper and tied it with a ribbon four feet wide and a hundred yards long, like a huge Christmas gift. (These true memories will seem more made up than some of my lies.) Another Christmas Uncle Bud climbed into his magnolia tree with a brush and a bucket of red paint and, in a certain pattern, painted all the leaves red so that the magnolia looked like a tree full of elephantine poinsettias. He drove his WWII Jeep with no top at breakneck speeds all over town, he gardened in his front yard in his jockey shorts, he came to track-and-field practices at the local high school and, wearing leather-soled dress shoes and a black suit and tie, outran our best sprinter in the hundred yard dash, and then did the same in the low hurdles. He raised hell, he delivered babies, he baked bread, he told wonderful stories, he built a medical clinic from lumber scraps salvaged from a WWII airbase that he personally tore down, board by board, himself. He even salvaged the old nails and reused them in the walls of the new clinic, and once let me pull a few nails out of the airbase walls with an instrument called a nail puller. Early in the century, when Uncle Bud was a teenager, his own father, my grandfather, also a physician, presented him with four thousand dollars to pay for his four years at Millsaps College in Jackson—it was a liberal sum at the time, and the idea of giving it to him in a lump was to teach him responsibility. My uncle spent every penny of this amount in his first semester at college and had to work at bad jobs for the rest of his college career to support himself. The world was my Uncle Bud's oyster. I longed for Uncle Bud to be my father. He is the original of the central character in my story "Storyteller," which ends with the storyteller befriending the alienated Hydro as if Hydro were his own son. This is the fantasy I had for myself with Uncle Bud.

Even many years later, when I was grown and had children of my own and my stepfather was dead, and Uncle Bud's wife, my Aunt Frances, died, I could not keep from wishing that somehow, in this liberal modem age of ours—it was the 1970s after all—he and my mother could finally be married, as I continued to believe they should have done all along. Shall I confess, too, that I actually suggested this ridiculous notion to my mother in the car on the day of Aunt Frances' funeral and that my mother was quite horrified? This was the extent of my great continuing deep need—longing is the only word that seems sufficient—for a proper father to fill some incredible void left in me by my natural father's death. Never once before the day that I am writing this could I have known, seen clearly and been able to put to words, these feelings, and I am not much embarrassed that now they appear, even to me, a little pathetic, not to mention a little bizarre.

So if I were to make a guess at the origins of my persistent pursuit of the theme of unfulfilled dreams of romance, particularly regarding fathers and sons, I suspect it would not reside simply in the fact that I was sometimes disappointed in my expectations of my stepfather, but because before this man who eventually married my mother was ever introduced to my mother, my fantasy of the possibilities of fatherhood were already so enormous, so, in fact, fantastic, so impossibly romantic, so entirely pornographic (since they were based upon the seductive dazzle and glitter of larger-than-life parts and not on anything complex or coherent or realistic in terms of actual human relationships), no man on earth, let alone some housepainter in Itta Bena, Mississippi, could have ever lived up to them.

So I am saying I think I have run to ground the bad fox of my fictions, the elusive theme of foiled expectations and spoiled romance.

And yet I began by saying that these fictions are so much a part of me that I scarcely know which are true and which are not. Many times I have claimed that my stories were autobiographical in detail when most assuredly they were not. I wasn't lying. I thought these things happened to me. I thought I jumped on a freight train and rode many miles. I thought I fished for chickens. I thought I was given a funny sex education lecture. But to imagine that written down stories are somehow history as well is not so surprising, I think. It's easy enough to believe that an author lives with characters for a while and then takes them on in the way an actor takes on a role he or she is playing. There is nothing so amazing about this.

But what about those stories that were not written? What about those nonevents that I have told and repeated as my history, such as the hunting trip I never went on? What in the world are they all about?

The fact is I have been making up lies—lies that I believed myself— for as long as can remember. A great central core of these lies involves my stepfather. And not all of them are structured around expectation and disappointment.

Some of them are simply lies. I told a group of kids in college that my father—stepfather, of course, though I never mentioned this—had his PhD in chemistry from the University of Michigan. In fact my father— stepfather—was a housepainter who was sent by the army to Ann Arbor to a six-week school to study how to paint ammunition. "That's the closest I ever came to going to college," he once told me, and so paint and chemicals and college and Dad were from that moment woven into a weird fabric in my mind that emerged as a degree in chemistry. And a PhD, no less!

Another time I said—(and remember, I believed this)—that he was an artist, and strongly implied that he specialized in art restoration in stonework. In fact, he once touched up, rather skillfully apparently, some old paint work on a fireplace—and so that's where I got the art restoration and stonework angle. I said—believed!—that he dated a midget. I said this because he lived for a while in Sarasota, Florida, near the home of the winter circus. I said that he died beneath our house and had to be pulled out by a rope tied around his feet.

Let me slow down for a minute on this one. This one is complicated. I never actually believed that my father died under our house or that I pulled him out with a rope. I was once in a conversation with the author Otto Salassi, who when asked about his father, said, "He's dead." Otto Salassi's father was in fact not dead, but a father character in a book Otto had just written had died (beneath a house, actually). At the time Otto caught himself and laughed and said, "Actually my father is not dead. My character just died." I was envious of an author who could so completely identify with characters he had created, and so in later conversations, I said that my own father had actually died under our house. Then just as Otto Salassi had done, I laughed and caught myself in the "mistake" and made the correction. So, the truth is, I didn't ever believe that my father died under the house but I did believe that I had originally said that he did. Or to put it another way, I magically turned into Otto Salassi long enough to make Otto's mistake, and to correct the mistake in Otto's easy way, and so, with my stepfather's help, I became an author-type person who could make such a mistake. Jeeziz!

You could conclude from all this that my inventions are somehow a predictable bit of lying for the usual purposes of lying—to gain something, or to hurt someone else. I could gain status among my friends by being the kind of cool guy who has an artist or chemistry teacher for a father, or the kind of into-it-all-the-way writer who confuses fact and fiction, and I could hurt my father's memory by implying that he was a redneck or a fool. There is no point in denying that these are my probable motives. But there is another part of this as well. In all my inventions and fictions, those for publication and those to impress or amuse my friends, I have been doing one thing. This part was only for myself. Not to hurt others or to impress my friends. I have been inventing a father. It was a way of inventing myself—my self.

Without a father I was intolerable to myself. Without a father I was not a person worthy of my own regard. For all my life it has been unacceptable to me that I could not have the father that death took from me, or if not him then the father of my fantasy, the one I made up from selected detail from the life of my Uncle Bud. I have strayed from that original invention, I have added details of intimacy and normalcy and loving support, and even political liberalism. I have attributed pithy sayings to my invented father: "I'm all for the two party system, except for the Republicans," I have falsely reported him to say. In this incarnation my father sounds like Will Rogers.

No matter to me. Consistency has not been a priority in this invention. I was determined to have a father, and so I have invented one out of the man whom I was given. I have made his imperfect flesh beautiful, his imperfect job exciting, he has become an excellent dancer, he is ironic and accepting of me, and if I am hurting and angry at the world, then I am angry at him and I make him a redneck. What is important, personally and in my life as a fiction writer, is that I have suffered from the belief that since I could not have the father that I first wanted, then I had no father at all, not unless I made him up myself and convinced the world and myself of the fact of him, the truth of him. Only in this way could I then begin to exist.

I have been inventing my father and his love—which I have not believed existed either, of course—and even my love for him—for a very long time. I repeat the same pattern many times: through tribulations I learn that my father is an exceptional man and that he loves me, despite many indications to the contrary. In life I never believed that my stepfather loved me in this way because I believed I could never love him in this way.

Even in my dreams I invented our love affair. I have a recurring dream in which the two of us fish together. The fish he catches are beautiful and cold and silver, the fish I catch are dwarfish, horrible little humanoids. In the end of the dream my father cooks and eats all the fish as if they were all beautiful, mine as well as his, and I feel well loved and fully accepted.

Later, in stories, I invented the same system. The structure of these stories often relies on the thwarting of expectation, but this is not all they are about. Sugar's father in "The All-Girl Football Team" accepts his son utterly, even the scary female part of him, and of himself, which perhaps I have had a hard time accepting in myself. The same in "Sugar Among the Chickens." His father believes in Sugar, believes that he will never be a fool to the things the father has been a fool to, marriage and geography and alcohol. The same in story after story. And so what is on the surface, so often, a story about the defeat of romantic expectation is in fact a triumph of romance.

For me personally anyway, if not for my fiction or for any reader who ever reads my work. I'm not bragging about my fiction here. What I have gained personally has little to do with the fiction that has more or less incidentally been produced. It is the invention of the father I always wanted, imperfect and yet perfect in all the right ways as well. Sugar is disappointed that he missed the freakshow, but he loves having a father who knew W. C. Handy, the Father of the Blues. Sugar is proud of his own father's freakishness, his webbed feet and rock 'n' roll suit, his love affair with a midget, his friendship with a wild roving band of eunuchs who clatter across bridges in the Delta flatscape looking for Episcopalians. (I'm tempted to say that these are the kinds of details that might actually have been true of Uncle Bud, though I suppose even Uncle Bud could not have actually known the magical eunuchs.) All I mean is, I never believed I had a father and so I invented the one I wanted, and in the process I invented Sugar and

I seem also to have invented myself. I did this without knowing I was doing anything at all. What I have done through intuition is probably listed somewhere in Darwinism under the title Odd Adaptations.

This new self, the one with nonevents in his life more important than actual historical events, is a person I have grown to like. The more of these inventions that have become a part of me—even now that I am coming clean about them as inventions—the more attractive I am to people who know me, the more confident I am of handling difficult situations (since a cool guy who has had all these experiences could never be frightened of, say, job interviews or women or surly contractors or whoever, whereas a guy who didn't have a father and was not loved might panic and not know what to say and nobody would like him and he would be a dweeb). There are a great many advantages to the invented father, the invented life.

And I suppose there will be advantages to the deinvention as well. It must be true, mustn't it, that in Darwinism one of the items under Odd Adaptations is not only Invention of Self Through Invention of Father, but also Discovery of the Real Self?

Maybe not. Probably the real self is in fact the invented self fully accepted. Always my stepfather will have been a housepainter and always, for one frightening moment in the Snack Shop on North State Street in Jackson, Mississippi, he will have had a doctorate in chemistry from the University of Michigan, and always my stepfather will have been a man who had a stepson who became a literary person and tried to give order to chaos, first by stretching history's boundaries to include what never happened, and then by shrinking them to acknowledge the lie, and then to say, with a conflicted heart, that since the nonhistorical was for a while historical then it too, in some way, must be included within history's elastic frame.

Lewis Nordan
Pittsburgh, 1991

STEVE WILSON

Lewis Nordan is the author of six other books of fiction, including the acclaimed novels *Wolf Whistle*, *The Sharpshooter Blues*, and *Lightning Song*, and a memoir, *Boy with Loaded Gun*. His many awards include three American Library Association Notable Book Citations, the Mississippi Institute of Arts and Letters Award for fiction, the Mississippi Authors Award for fiction, and the Southern Book Critics Circle Award for fiction. He died in 2012.

# Additional Books by Lewis Nordan
Available in Print and E-book Wherever Books Are Sold

### *Lightning Song,* a novel

When twelve-year-old Leroy Dearman's Uncle Harris arrives, life on the family llama farm takes on an entirely different flavor. Equilibrium tilts, lightning strikes, and Leroy finds himself kissing his innocence good-bye.

"*Portnoy's Complaint* set on a llama farm in Mississippi." —*Self* magazine

Fiction • Paperback edition: ISBN 978-1-56512-220-8 • E-book edition: ISBN 978-1-56512-764-7

### *The Sharpshooter Blues,* a novel

One fateful day in the Delta town of Arrow Catcher, an orphaned teen, known as The Sharpshooter, shows off his fancy moves at the William Tell grocery, but when Hydro Raney, the sweet, simple hero of the book, tries his hand, the results are cataclysmic.

"This is not just a good book, this is a marvelous book."
—*Voice Literary Supplement*

Fiction • Paperback edition: ISBN 978-1-56512-182-9 • E-book edition: ISBN 978-1-56512-886-6

### *Wolf Whistle,* a novel

When Lewis Nordan unleashed his extraordinary writing powers on the events surrounding the killing of Emmett Till and the subsequent trial during which his killers were acquitted by an all-white jury, the result was epic: profoundly sad, manically comic, and stunningly powerful.

"*Wolf Whistle* is an immense and wall-shattering display of talent."
—Randall Kenan, *The Nation*

"An illuminating, even uplifting, achievement . . . Flat-out wonderful."
—*The Washington Post Book World*

Fiction • Paperback edition: ISBN 978-1-56512-110-2 • E-book edition: ISBN 978-1-56512-913-9

# Other Lewis Nordan E-books

## *Sugar Among the Freaks,* stories

Fifteen stories for which the incomparable Lewis Nordan has plundered his own prodigiously rich stores of imagination and memory to give birth to his magnificent—and ongoing—creation, the mythical town of Arrow Catcher, Mississippi.

"Mr. Nordan's stories are splendid." —*The New York Times Book Review*

Stories • E-book edition: ISBN 978-1-56512-843-9

## *Boy with Loaded Gun,* a memoir

"The Huck Finn–like tale of an irresistible oddball turns into a heartrending account . . . A must for fans of Nordan's quirky fiction." —*Entertainment Weekly*

"The best thing Nordan's ever written. It's also the most honest, painful, unexpected and powerful sharing of a life." —*The Jackson (MS) Clarion-Ledger*

"Tracking a wild youth to a redeemed adulthood via a hilarious, tragic path, *Boy with Loaded Gun* is a spiritual autobiography about a determined kid forging an identity in a confusing world . . . Your own life may seem more incredible after you read it, your vision of what it means to be alive never quite the same." —*Men's Journal*

Memoir • E-book edition: ISBN 978-1-61620-460-0